ONE

GOOD

HUSTLE

ONE
GOOD
HUSTLE

A NOVEL

BILLIE
LIVINGSTON

 RANDOM HOUSE CANADA

PUBLISHED BY RANDOM HOUSE CANADA

Copyright © 2012 Billie Livingston

Published in 2012 by Random House Canada, a division of Random House of Canada Limited, Toronto. Distributed in Canada by Random House of Canada Limited.

www.randomhouse.ca

Random House Canada and colophon are registered trademarks.

LIBRARY AND ARCHIVES CANADA CATALOGUING IN PUBLICATION

Livingston, Billie, 1965–
  One good hustle : a novel / by Billie Livingston.

Issued also in electronic format.

ISBN 978-0-307-35988-9

  I. Title.

PS8573.I916O64 2012   C813'.54   C2011-907803-1

Cover images: (tracks) Alan Powdrill / Getty Images, (girl) Joerg Buschmann / Millennium Images, UK, (hair) doglikehorse / shutterstock.com

Printed and bound in the United States of America

10 9 8 7 6 5 4 3 2 1

For Sweet Timothy, my believer

ONE

THERE IS PROBABLY at least one good con for a situation like this, one decent, well-executed hustle that would turn the whole scene to my advantage. But I just can't think straight lately. Feels as if I've been beating my brains out forever, just trying to get an edge. Like a total amateur.

Jill's mom, Ruby, watches me with a closed-mouth smile—almost a smirk from where I'm sitting. We're in the basement, in Jill's bedroom, but Jill isn't here. The second that Ruby pushed through the beaded curtain in the doorway, Jill buggered off upstairs. Obviously a trap.

Ruby is sitting on Jill's bed now, one hand on either knee, her palms up like Buddha's mother. She's probably only forty but her hair is steel grey and she's built like a chubby bulldog. She's wearing this long, drapey vest-thing over stretchy black pants, which reminds me of Bea Arthur as Maude, except Ruby's about half Bea Arthur's height. Clearly Jill got her gargantuan size from her father's side of the family.

I tilt up the corners of my mouth but keep it shut. Ruby keeps on smiling, gives me a slow easy blink. This is no staring contest. It's more like a game of inscrutable chicken.

Finally she exhales through her nose and says, "Well, Sammie, you've been sleeping in our basement for two weeks and no one knows why."

I nod at the floor. She's got a point. I've been hogging half of Jill's bed now for two weeks exactly. I hadn't meant to. I kept hoping my dad might show up and I'd get out of here before anyone knew what hit them. Fat chance. Sam's nowhere to be seen. I've got noplace else to go and Ruby's got me cornered. Sam once said, if you think you got to fight to win then you're an amateur. "That's the difference between us and them," he said. "The professional works out everything that the amateur has to sweat out. If you got to sweat every move, that's what you call a rough hustle." He told my mother that shortly before he got arrested and did two years for grand larceny and contributing to the delinquency of a minor. I was the minor. I didn't have to do any time, though. I was only eight.

"Yup," I finally say out loud. Ruby keeps gawking at me, waiting for an explanation. What does she expect? I can't rat out my mother.

If I don't say *something*, though, she might turf me.

"It's my mom." Fill in the blanks yourself.

That is the heart of it, after all. My mother. Marlene's been the problem for a while. Seems impossible when I think of how just a couple of years ago Marlene was a fucking force of nature! I suppose she always drank a little, but not like this. She was sharp. I told her everything. We trusted each other like crazy. She drilled it into my head that once you catch a person in a lie, it's hard to ever trust that person again. By "person," she meant me. Us. Everyone else was grey area.

Nowadays, living with Marlene—talk about your rough hustles. She doesn't even *try* to act decent any more. I *am* sixteen, though. Only one more year until I graduate. Four months after that, I'll be legal. At midnight, on November 2, 1985, I will be eighteen years old. Until two weeks ago, I thought I could stick it out.

Ruby watches me. She's waiting for the rest.

"I couldn't stay," I tell her. "She's . . . you know."

Forget it. I'm not saying more. I barely even know Jill, never mind her mother. Jill and I only started hanging out a few months ago. She knows I was named after my father and that he doesn't pay child support. And that Marlene thinks Sam's a major prick. That's about it, really. She doesn't know what kind of people I come from.

"She's not feeling well. Flu." I gaze up at Jill's framed *Foxy Brown* movie poster, on the wall behind Ruby—Pam Grier in a long black wig with a little silver gun on her ankle. All around her a dozen little Pams beat the shit out of bad guys. *Don't mess aroun' with . . . Foxy Brown. She's the meanest chick in town.* I'd never heard of this movie before I knew Jill.

"Sammie," Ruby calls me back. "Are you saying something?"

I must've been moving my lips as I read. Ruby ducks her head, trying to make eye contact, but I'm not into it. I don't want to deal with Ruby. I start fidgeting with the beanbag chair—the orange leather is peeling like bad sunburn.

"Tell me about your mom. Has she been hurting you?"

My eyes jerk up. *Hurting?* Does she mean hitting? "Shit, I could take my mother," I blurt. Stupid thing to say. I'm stupid. "No. It's *her*. She wants to, like"—I look back at Foxy, the silver gun on her ankle—"hurt *herself*. She wants to kill herself."

Ruby's skinny, pencilled eyebrows rise.

I feel like a fink—but really, it's barely anything, what I told. It's not like it's illegal to have suicidal thoughts. Part of me is relieved. The rest is embarrassed like I just coughed up phlegm. Except it's not my phlegm and I have no right coughing it up.

"I offered to help," I add. "No, I mean . . ."

Ruby's eyes are sympathetic all of a sudden. I have just become a pathetic little splotch on her daughter's beanbag chair: some poor, sticky welfare kid with a mother who plans to off herself.

Regular Ruby and her regular husband, Lou, in their regular house with their regular pickup truck. What's a Regular Ruby supposed to think of a situation like this?

I look at her. She has pink blusher on her freckled cheeks and stubby mascaraed eyelashes that I can just make out in the dim light of Jill's hanging paper lantern. Jill told me once that her parents were real partiers until they became Christians. Then they gave up drinking and settled right down. It is a fact that I have not seen Ruby or Lou drink since I've been here, but I haven't seen anyone go to church either.

It's probably true, though. I'm a total magnet for Jesus freaks. My best friend Drew is a Jesus freak but we haven't spoken since I took off. He probably hates me now. Christian or not, you can only turn your other cheek for so damn long.

"She's depressed," I explain to Ruby. "She always talks about it. She's tried it a couple of times. Sort of. So, when she told me she was definitely going to do it, I offered to help her get pills. But I said I wasn't going to watch."

Ruby winces and I go back to picking the orange skin on the beanbag chair. "Yeah," I say, and suddenly I'm goofing with the ditzy hippie-voice that Jill and I like to do. "Like, a totally bad scene, baby. Not cool."

Ruby just sits, her stubby little hands on her knees. She has three rings on one and two on the other. I can hear Marlene sing the way she did when I was a kid: *"With rings on her fingers and bells on her toes, she shall have music wherever she goes!"*

I don't believe that my mother will actually kill herself. But I'm not telling Ruby that. Or the fact that I sort of wish she would. We really are fucked up, Marlene and me. There's no greeting card for a case like us.

Ruby lifts her hands off her knees, laces her fingers and looks into the empty bowl of her palms. *Here is the church, here is the steeple,* I think. *Open the doors and where are the people?*

She lets a slow sigh go. "When's the last time you saw her?"

"A few days ago. I had to pick up some more clothes. She asked me to get her some stuff at the store."

5

Her eyebrows angle up again, then her mouth gets thin and hard and she gives me one of those solid looks of determination that grown-ups sport on kids' TV. I can see now why little kids might like that sort of thing. It's confidence building.

"Did you know we used to run a group home here, Sammie?"

I nod. Jill talks about those days sometimes, the harsh chicks and guys who used to stay here, prosti-tots and pickpockets. Jill told me that if one of those girls heard that a new guy was coming to the house, she'd go stand outside on the porch so that her nipples would get hard from the cold. I didn't get it. Jill explained that it was so the guy would get turned on at the sight of her and then nipple-chick would be first in line for his weed or whatever he was carrying. I found that hard to believe. Jill put her hand on her hip, pushed her fat lips out at me and said, "Look, baby, I know more about sex and drugs than you'll know in a lifetime." Jill would kill to be a black chick. Pam Grier.

"Do you want to stay on here for a while?" Ruby says.

I take a breath and look her in the eyes for as long as I can stand it.

"All right," she says. "We need to set up an appointment with a worker at Social Services. And someone needs to check in on your mother. I'll get Lou to take me over there when he gets off work tomorrow."

When she catches my expression, Ruby gives me a tough sort of chuckle. "We just want to notify Social Services of the situation. If Lou and I are on the record as your temporary guardians, they'll send support cheques so we can afford to feed you."

Anyone can weasel her way around a social worker. But wait till Ruby gets a load of Marlene. And vice versa. I open my mouth to protest but there's no point. It's her own fault—Marlene's got it coming.

TWO

THIS IS THE LAST DAY of grade 11. One more year and I'm finished. Forever. I'm pretty sure my dad is a high-school dropout. Maybe it didn't matter as much forty years ago. But nowadays, "high-school dropout" sounds lame. And kind of skeevy.

I stare up at the clock. 2:15.

A monitor walks up and down the aisles, watching us. Not our regular English teacher. She taps the desk of one girl, two rows over: *Eyes on your own paper.*

I'm sitting here in room 221 doing my final English exam and all I can think of is Ruby and Lou descending on Marlene.

I wrote down the phone number for Ruby this morning.

"We'll just look in on her, make sure she's all right," she said. Ruby was stern but energetic about it all.

Being looked in on goes against everything Marlene stands

for. Unless it's a guy. If Lou was going over on his own, Marlene would be all for it.

Lou's shift is the early one: 5:30 a.m. to 1 p.m. He works as a guard at Oakalla Prison Farm here in Burnaby. Jill's dad is the opposite of my dad in just about every way you can think of. They're both quiet, but that's where the similarity ends. Lou is so tall he has to duck his head to come into a room; Sam claims he's 5-foot-10 but he says a lot of things. Lou wears a close-cropped beard, I think to hide his pockmarks; Sam's got no facial hair, I think so a potential mark will believe Sam's got nothing to hide. Jill gets her jollies when people mistake her for Lou's girlfriend instead of his daughter. Nobody would ever mistake Sam and me for a couple.

Wait till Marlene gets a gander at giant Lou. She's probably staring at him right now. It's hard to know with Marlene if she'll get scared, or turned on.

At two-thirty I'm out the door. I love these final exam days. You just get up and walk out when you're done. And English exams—I mean, for chrissake, if you have two brain cells to rub together, how can you not pass an English test? Mind you, I probably wouldn't have said that a few weeks ago when I kept walking into things. Forgetting what I was saying and where I was going. Wondering if Marlene would still be breathing when I got home.

It got so bad that Mr. Walters, my Trades Math teacher, asked if he could speak to me after class. It's a bit embarrassing that I take Trades Math, but when things started to get hairy at home I didn't want to take the chance of failing geometry or trigonometry or whatever else they were selling. I just wanted a class that would show me how to think on my feet, keep my funds in order. Sam would approve, I figured. My dad is a practical sort of guy.

Mr. Walters, who is also one of the school's two guidance counsellors, waited until the classroom was empty before he got serious with me.

"Everything okay?" he asked.

Without those student bodies filling up space, the words echoed off all Walters' little chalk numbers on the blackboard. He'd been talking about taxes, I think. Or the way compound interest is calculated daily—something useful, but I couldn't concentrate. Walters had a very concerned expression on his face and his long eyebrows pricked up like antennae.

I waited for some smart-assed response to come out of me. Nothing. Blank. So I shrugged.

"I know I should be grateful for small mercies," he said, "but you didn't say a word today. You stared right through me. Frankly, you have me a little worried."

Generally speaking, Mr. Walters is an easy target. Short, with a face like a penguin and a persnickety, anxious demeanour, he's the sort of guy whose pants you want to pull down just before you leave him blindfolded on the front stoop of a convent.

The fact that he wanted to know why I was too depressed to harass him seemed pathetic and beautiful all at once. I was scared I might start bawling. I wished I could hug him. I wished that he would hug me and pat my back with nice quiet thumps, the way Marlene used to do when I skinned the crap out of my knee.

What I really wished was that I could just tell on her. What would a proper little guy like Mr. Walters think if he knew that the night before, my mother had sat on the couch putting on her makeup because she was planning to off herself?

"I'm going to throw myself off a pier," Marlene had said, and then she put more lipstick on. My mother has always liked the idea of looking pretty when she dies. So she kept at it, putting on layer after layer of mascara while she talked about how she would dive into the ocean. "My bones drifting free, finally free," she said, as if it was the most gorgeous ambition ever.

In other words, I thought, you want to be a jellyfish, one of those floating, white ballerina-things that dance in the quietest parts of the water.

She caught me rolling my eyes.

"You know *everything*, don't you." She took another slug of her vodka and milk, zipped up her makeup bag, and announced that she was going to jump off the roof of our building instead.

I didn't respond. I was at the dinner table, trying to finish a short story for English class. Coming from a family of bullshit artists, fiction is the only school thing I truly excel at.

"So s-superior . . ." Marlene sputtered. "I was going to get you some bubbly for your sweet sixteenth, a nice little bottle of Baby Duck maybe. But you'd have turned your nose up at *that!*"

"My body is a temple," I said.

"Oh, for chrissake! Why couldn't you just turn Catholic like a normal person?"

It's because of Marlene that I even *know* any born-again-Christian kids. I wouldn't know a guy like Drew, that's for sure, except that Marlene had the bright idea to send me to camp a couple of summers ago so she and Fat Freddy could take off for a week and work a few hustles in Los Angeles. It turned out to be one of those Jesus camps. The Welfare paid for it. Most of the camps Welfare pays for are Jesus camps. It's like they think that poor kids must all be morally bankrupt too.

The Hollow Tree Ranch was set up like the Old West and the pastor who ran the campground called himself Tex. I thought I'd died and gone to hell, sitting in the chapel the first morning, listening to Tex spout off about what it means to "put a spoke in the devil's wheels."

I pulled a pen out of my purse. I had bought a postcard in the tuck shop and I was about to write an earful to Marlene about where she'd sent me. From my left I could feel a pair of eyes watching my hands. It was the guy I'd noticed when I arrived the afternoon before. He was gangly, with woolly blond hair and a sweet face, and he sang so loud at the first evening campfire that I thought he had to be joking. I turned my head and stared him in the eye. He smiled and looked away. Christian wimp, I thought.

I left the postcard in my purse and, instead, carefully drew a pentagram on my palm. The wimp blinked down at my hand. I wiggled my fingers in his direction and gave him a wink. He hiccuped, suppressing a giggle. That was Drew.

"You're bad," he whispered. Eyes twinkling, he looked almost giddy.

"You ain't seen nothin' yet."

"I can't wait." He grinned.

We were inseparable for the rest of the week. I wished we went to the same school but Drew's family lived in North Burnaby while Marlene and I lived in South. Maybe he was a church guy but he wasn't super pious or anything, just kind of abnormally clean-living. Which suited me fine because I'm abnormal too. If I were normal, I wouldn't be a virgin who doesn't drink or smoke.

After our Hollow Tree Ranch week, Drew invited me to some of his church's DYF nights. DYF stands for Divine Youth Fellowship—Tenth Avenue Divine is the name of Drew's church. They have these roller parties the first Friday of every month. I went with him to a DYF roller party once. At the rink, I said "shit" when I landed on my ass and Mandy Peterson, one of the DYFers, looked at me like I'd just ripped off a big fart.

"I used to swear," Mandy said to me. "People underestimated me when I swore."

I didn't fit in but at least nobody wanted to beat me up. They were nice to me. Even that Mandy Peterson chick was nice. Especially when I tried not to swear.

The DYFers had a game night at Mandy's house once. Her parents had a nice place: tons of bedrooms, two cars and a boat. Those church kids all seemed to have boats and swimming pools and camping equipment and rumpus rooms and chandeliers. Marlene asked me once if I felt bad being in their houses, uncomfortable, like I didn't belong there. I think she was trying to ask if I felt low-class next to them. I was too busy swimming in their pools and eating steak off their fancy plates. Deluxe accommodations suited me just fine. And to be honest, the whole clean-living thing gave me a weird, spearmint-fresh feeling inside. All that chastity stuff was kind of a relief after years of Marlene.

One time, a year or so ago, I was complaining about my zits. Marlene was acting all ballsy and sexy with a vodka brave-on. She told me I should go get laid and my skin would clear right up.

That's when I told her that I was going to save myself until marriage.

"Over my dead body!" she said. "You want to end up with some guy who does a wham-bam-thank-you-ma'am and then leaves you lying there? Staring at the ceiling? Stuck with him? *Married* to him?"

"God! There's other stuff, you know. Ways of knowing that someone would be nice to you in bed."

"*Other* stuff? Those goddamn Christians are going to ruin your life."

Treat your body as a temple, the youth pastor would tell us. I started tossing that one at Marlene to get a rise out of her. Drove her bats. *Holier than thou sons-of-bitches,* she'd say.

It pisses me off when Marlene slags all that religious stuff as being totally not like us—I suppose because I'm scared she's right. I mean, why *is* Drew friends with me? Maybe he's only nice to me because he *has* to be—it's in the Bible. Meanwhile, I don't know if I even believe in God.

At the Jesus camp, they sang this song that went, *I've got the joy joy joy down in my heart.* I don't think I have that. I know my mother doesn't.

From the corner of my eye, I saw her turn around on the couch and stare at me. "I love you, you know," she said. "More than anything in the world."

I wanted to pound her. Instead, in this very matter-of-fact way, I asked, "How're you going to get on the roof?"

She blinked. "Fine. I'll go up to the top floor and jump off someone's balcony." She pulled her purse straps over her shoulder, stood up, and went strutting down the hallway like it was a red carpet.

"Yeah?" I followed her. "Who'd let *you* in?"

"That won't be hard." She opened the front door of our apartment and tossed me a creepy starlet glance over her shoulder. "I'll just smile." Her teeth flashed.

I watched her head down the hall and push the elevator button. She waved to me as she got on. I slammed the apartment door.

Do it, then. See if I care.

I wandered into her room. The top drawer in her dresser was open—that's where she keeps her stash. I plucked out a prescription bottle: Valium 10mg. When I turned it over, all the little blue happy pills rattled around. Actually, "happy pills" is a misnomer. They're "I-don't-give-a-crap pills." She'd become a big fan of Ativan too. Same shit.

I read once about this woman who took Valium before she cut her wrists and bled to death in a nice hot bath. Does blood look beautiful when you're stoned on Valium? In the dresser mirror, my pupils were holes in my head. Little black monsters stared out of them. I pushed my hair out of my face. All the cool girls at school seem to have smooth TV hair, but mine is a frizzy, curly, snaky mess. The day I first talked to Drew, he said, "Man, I love your hair—it's that wild witchy hippie kind of hair." He *loved* it, he said. I started to not mind my head so much after that. Drew likes when I wear drapey hippie blouses too. I have lots of those now.

I don't know how long I stood there thinking about that sort of stuff, but when I heard the front door opening, I dropped the Valium back in her drawer. I went into the living room as Marlene came waltzing in, all giddy and grinning. Turned out she'd never made it to the roof. She'd been hanging out with the goof upstairs, the unemployed guy with the moustache who lies around on his balcony all day, tanning. I went to my bedroom and closed the door.

———

I didn't tell Mr. Walters any of that, though. I told him I had insomnia. It wasn't a lie either. I had been awake till one or two in the morning trying to think of quick and easy ways to die: eating Drano (in gel capsules so it'd just slip down), electrocution (blow-dryer in the bathtub), fast-moving truck (stepping in front of). One time on *The Phil Donahue Show,* I saw a woman tell the whole world how her son died by auto-erotic asphyxiation. He hanged himself with a necktie in his closet, accidentally suffocating while he jerked off over a porn mag.

How can you tell a guidance counsellor shit like that? You'd sound like a whiny pathetic jerk, snivelling for attention. Sam says that serious people don't talk, they act.

But after I left Walters that day, I was pissed off that I couldn't say anything to him. I'm pretty sure that is when I first started to actually *plan* Marlene's suicide. She could wash a couple of Valium down with vodka. Maybe she'd forget and I'd give her a couple more. When she passed out, I could lay the pillow on her face and slowly push down. What would be so wrong about it? She kept on insisting she wanted to die, and I could help. I could be the one to make things right for her. I started to think that this was the only way out for Marlene and me. She couldn't bear to be alive and I couldn't bear to watch her misery any more. I would be a strange kind of angel.

But I had to figure out the money situation. I'd need enough to get me through for the first few weeks at least.

What if I endorsed the welfare cheque over to me when it came? Or I could deposit the cheque into her account and write myself a new one.

I couldn't stop thinking how it would work.

I remember it was one-thirty in the morning and I was in my room, sitting up in bed, practising Marlene's signature in my school binder. I had started by tracing her name from an old cancelled cheque. Then I went freehand. I'd done two nearly full pages of *Marlene Bell, Marlene Bell* . . .

It was quiet that night. No sirens in the distance. No voices in the halls.

17

I thought I heard muttering and I glanced at the wall that separated our bedrooms. It almost sounded as though she was crying. Then nothing.

I went back to my signatures.

A screech ripped the air.

Jolting up from the page, I knocked my head against the wall. *Marlene.*

I stared at the wall between our rooms again. Her scream became a crying wail and I ripped the signature pages out of my binder and crumpled them up. I switched off my lamp and stared into the dark, my heart banging away like a monkey in a cage.

The wailing turned into loud gasping sobs and I jumped out of bed just as my mother's door flung open. I heard her stagger against the wall as she rushed toward the kitchen. I chased after her.

As I came round the corner, she pulled a butcher knife out of the sink. In just her bra and panties, she turned the point of the blade toward her stomach. Then she let it drop.

"It's too dirty," she said. She sank to the floor, choking on her tears. "And I'm too fat. It'll never go in. How did I get so fat?"

I tried to help her up, but she pushed me away.

I went back into my room, took the crumpled pages out of the wastebasket and ripped them into pieces and more pieces. Miserable confetti.

The next morning while she was sleeping, I got up the guts to phone my dad in Toronto. We hadn't heard from him in months. I thought maybe if Sam knew how shitty things were, he would come and get us.

Sitting in the living room I filled him in as quietly as I could. "She threatened to stab herself in the stomach last night. Last *week* she swallowed a bottle of pills and then called the ambulance. Another time she said she was going to drown herself." I had decided before I picked up the phone that there was not going to be any crying, but that went out the window as soon as I heard Sam's voice. "I can't stay here," I said.

It was silent on his end. I waited for him to say something. Something about a plane ticket for me.

"I'm goin' out of town," he blurted. "You got friends you could stay with?"

Not much to talk about after that.

When I came home from school to pack my bag before going to stay with Jill, Marlene came into my bedroom and sat on the floor with her back to the wall, tears rolling.

"I just can't—" She wiped her nose with a Kleenex. "I don't know how to fill another day. It's such a relief to go to sleep and so horrible when I wake up and know I have to drag through another one, like a thousand pounds of dead . . . until I can sleep again."

I sat on the edge of my bed and watched her. Mascara had streaked down her cheeks into the corners of her mouth. She dug her fingers into my bedroom rug.

"I wanted you to know because—" She swallowed. "I always thought it was cruel when I heard a woman killed herself and let her kids find her like that. I didn't want that."

I said, "If you want help trying to get pills together, I'll try. But, um, I have to go. I'm not going to watch."

I couldn't look at her. I kept tweetzing the sheet on my bed. Tweetzing is this thing I do where I rub a fold of the cotton between my fingers. Marlene says I've been doing it since I was a baby.

I nodded to myself. "I can't be here for—" I lost the words then, as if I had already begun to seep away, long before I stood up to leave.

THREE

JILL'S LAST EXAM was earlier in the day so she was long gone by the time I got out.

Except for Jill, I don't have a crowd at school. Part of the problem is, like my dad, I don't drink or smoke. Sam says addicts are weak. People in this school don't hold that opinion, though. The halls are full of alkies and heads who think the fact that I don't drink or smoke weed means I'm a spineless little suck. A chick named Crystal Norris actually shoulder-checked me in the hall once and called me a suckhole. I didn't do anything about it so maybe she had a point.

When I come through the front door, I hear Jill squeal, "She said what?" Jill's front door opens into a tiny vestibule with a few coat hooks. Two steps forward and you're in the living room.

Creeping onto the braided rug, I pause, listening as Jill and Ruby cackle in the kitchen. The hair on my arms prickles.

They're talking about Marlene. I know it. Laughing at her.

I keep still, listening as I glance around. There are two little paintings on the wall over the couch: a happy clown and a sad clown. I hate those clowns. Even the happy one looks miserable.

The furniture is old, but everything's tidy. Clean. Maybe some dust on the TV screen but that's about it. Marlene likes to say, "I don't mind clutter but I hate dirt." What a laugh that is. My stomach lurches when I think of what Ruby and Lou probably saw over there today. At least Jill wasn't with them.

"She's a piece of work all right," I hear Ruby say.

"How did Dad react?"

It's quiet a moment. Ruby calls, "Sammie? That you?"

Shit. "Yeah," I yell through the wall at them.

When I come into the kitchen, Ruby and Jill are at the table, an ashtray and two cups of coffee between them. Smoke wafts out of Jill's mouth.

"Hey, sugar," she says. "What's shakin'?" Bright purple lipstick greases the filter of her cigarette.

"Nothin.' What's shakin' with you guys?"

"My thighs," Jill says. "Like a Jell-O tree in a windstorm."

That's a favourite line of Jill's. She probably says it five times a week.

Ruby titters and taps ash off her cigarette. "Were you eavesdropping, Sammie?"

My mouth opens. "Excuse me?"

Another one of Ruby's *gotchas*.

She bounces her skinny eyebrows. "You snuck through the front door like a cat burglar."

"No. I just dropped some stuff out of my purse so I was—"

Ruby laughs big. Making me squirm is a total riot, I guess.

Jill picks her compact up off the table. Gold bangles jangle up her arm as she checks out her purple lips in the mirror, snaps it shut. She drops the compact into her purse.

"Well, just so's you know, we have no secrets around here," Ruby says. "Sit down so we can talk about you to your face."

Jill laughs. She brushes some chalky face powder off the strained denim on her thigh. Her *thunder thighs,* she calls them. Jill is what Marlene would call "built." About five-foot-ten, she probably weights a hundred and sixty pounds. Boobs out to here, hips out to there. I look like a boy next to her.

"There's fresh coffee if you want," Jill tells me.

I go to the counter and pour a cup. I used to only drink tea but coffee's the thing around here.

"So, I met your mother today," Ruby says.

I sit down at the table with my mug and dump in extra sugar. Extra cream. I want extra everything lately.

"I called her before I went over and she didn't seem too interested in company." Ruby is wearing her ironic face.

"*Really?*" Jill slaps a hand to her chest for extra mock-value. "How strange!"

Ruby grins. "*Very strange.* I told her that we were worried."

I chew off a bit of skin inside my cheek and start in on my bottom lip.

"So, Lou and I went over there." Ruby takes a drag off her smoke and shakes her head as she exhales. "She hadn't bothered to get dressed. Just lay there in this old stained negligee, saying her head ached, her back ached, she couldn't find *Freddy*'s number—whoever that is—she had the shakes, she needed a drink. She actually asked Lou if he would pick her up something at the liquor store. She said she was scared of getting the DTs. Food didn't even occur to her. And *every*thing was filthy! Dirty dishes piled in the sink and on the counters. How she can live like that . . . or let her *daughter* live like that . . ." Ruby flicks her cigarette. "Poor Sammie."

My jaw clenches. "I was going to clean up," I say. "Before I left . . . Vacuum. And wash the—"

"Sammie, that was two weeks ago."

Stop saying my name. "So?"

"So, what self-respecting person—" Ruby stops. "Well, I guess that's the problem, she's not a self-respecting person. Or she wouldn't talk about killing herself when she has a daughter to look after." She sighs. "The sad thing is, she was probably a nice-looking woman at one point."

Probably? Fuck. "She's still—She's *depressed*."

Ruby pats my arm. "Sammie, she doesn't need your sympathy right now. You did her a big favour when you left."

Jill eyes me and plucks the gold chain off her chest, plays the little gold cross back and forth with a look that I can't make out.

"I guess you know she's drinking pretty hard," Ruby says. "There was an empty bottle on the coffee table. Nothing in the fridge but sour milk and some condiments. Mouldy bread on the counter. Pill bottles all over the place. I picked a prescription bottle up and she says to me, "Mind your own business, you tubby little dyke."

I choke back a laugh. Even fucked up, Marlene kicks ass.

Jill giggles and shakes her head theatrically. "Tubby little dyke," she repeats.

Ruby butts out her cigarette. "*Then* she started hitting on Lou."

Jill's eyes widen like she just can't believe it. I know the look on her face now—as if Marlene and I are on one of those TV shows with the white trash characters that make everyone giggle and gag.

"She says to him, 'What's a gorgeous hunk of man like you doing stuck with *that*.'" Ruby puts on a drunken, haughty face that looks nothing like Marlene's. "'Maybe you should come visit me on your own.'"

Jill says, "Wow. This chick is, like, not mellow at all."

Ruby joins in, mimicking the hippie-girl voice. "Totally *unmellow*."

I'm glad Marlene hit on Lou. Ruby asked for it. Tubby little dyke.

Ruby takes a fresh cigarette from her pack. Her face becomes suddenly stony as she says, "Seriously, though, Sammie, your mom's got problems." She lights the new smoke and thinks for a moment.

Still fiddling with her gold chain, Jill sets her elbows on the table, nudging the coffee cup with her boobs. "What did Dad say when she hit on him?"

"He said *no!*" Ruby eyeballs the ceiling and then looks back at me. "We did pick her up a few groceries. Milk and bread, cheese . . . Did you know your mom still holds a torch for your father?"

I huff through my nose. *As if!*

"Oh-ho, yes. She sure does."

Ruby doesn't know what the hell she's talking about. I am almost offended to think that Marlene is trying to find Fat Freddy's number, though. Freddy is the last thing she needs.

He called our place a couple months ago to ask if we'd seen Sam. "He was in town," Freddy said. "I thought sure he'd've called you!"

He knew damn well Sam never called us. He just wanted to rub it in, get even because Marlene had put him on the back burner again.

Now Marlene can't find his number. She must be really out of it. I don't want her calling Freddy. Is she planning to go work a few hustles with him? In the shape *she's* in? Or does she just want him to bring her a bottle? That weasel would only show up for one reason. The thought of any quid pro quo with Freddy makes me want to spew.

FOUR

FAT FREDDY IS a fence who used to work with Marlene and my dad back when we were a family. After Sam was out of the picture, Fat Freddy weaseled in close to Marlene. I'm not crazy about Freddy. I was happier when he was out of our world, even though she and Freddy used to make pretty good coin together when they ran the Birthday Girl Scam.

It worked like this. Marlene would sit at the bar in a hotel lounge. She'd order herself a drink and ask the bartender his name. Flashing some cash around ("Can you break a hundred?"), she'd say that it was her birthday. Then she'd confide that her boyfriend let her pick out her own present and she'd hold out her arm to show off her new diamond bracelet. The bartender might say, "Whoa, what'd that run the poor bastard?" She would scrunch up her nose when she whispered, *"Six thousand, two hundred, and twenty-five dollars!"*

Meanwhile, she'd actually bought it for six bucks off some street vendor.

When she finished her drink, she'd gather up her things and surreptitiously drop the bracelet under the bar stool. A few minutes later, Fat Freddy (it used to be my father) would walk in and take the seat Marlene had just left. Not long after that, Marlene would phone the bar, all frantic. The bartender would look for the bracelet. Freddy would move his foot—"You mean this?"

Freddy wouldn't hand the bracelet over. He'd just eyeball it and maybe whistle. "Ask if there's a reward," he'd say to the bartender.

On the phone, Marlene would cry. I watched her do it, watched her cradle the receiver as she pushed out tears, even though no one could see her. "I have to get that bracelet back. Please," she'd beg. "Tell him I'll give him a thousand dollars. Cash." Nearly every time, the bartender would hang up and haggle. He'd offer Freddy fifty bucks, imagining he'd pocket the difference when Marlene showed up with the thousand.

Freddy would laugh. "Forget it, man." He'd pocket the bracelet. "I gotta get goin.'"

The bartender would get anxious then, and Freddy could usually get him to fork over anywhere from two hundred to four hundred bucks. One time, he got five hundred.

Marlene said there was nothing wrong with a hustle like that because if the bartender hadn't been such a lying, cheating dirtbag in the first place, he'd never have given any money to Freddy. I always wondered about that reasoning, though. What if the bartender wasn't looking to pocket the difference? What if he was trying to help Marlene, the damsel in distress—save her from having to pay so much to the creepy guy holding her bracelet hostage? How could she know for sure?

But Marlene and Freddy's business partnership eventually soured. Fat Freddy had a major crush on Marlene. Something happened—I don't know what, but she made it clear that she wasn't into him. Freddy couldn't handle the rejection. He started to become undependable, standing her up when they had work planned. He'd claim she had her dates mixed up, but Freddy was full of shit and Marlene knew it.

Her One-Woman Hotel Hustle was born when she and Freddy were on hiatus.

When I was thirteen, I could still pass for a ten-year-old. I haven't got much up top even now but three years ago I was positively infantile. And Marlene had it in her head that she could pass me off as a little girl. Having a little girl, she figured, upped the ante as far as us being needy.

Marlene often drove us over the border into the States. Sometimes she'd do the little resort towns on the coast or maybe she'd hit Seattle, or Tacoma, or Portland. Now and then, she'd work downtown in Vancouver since, she reasoned, the marks would be from out of town.

If it was a big urban hotel, Marlene would sit in the lounge wearing her Chanel suit—this slim ivory number that managed to look very classy while still showing off her shape. She kept her ankles crossed and out to the side. Some guy once told Marlene that she had well-turned ankles, so she believed they were one of her most excellent features.

She'd have a suitcase beside her chair, a weepy look on her face and a tissue in hand to wipe her eyes.

Usually it went like this: A man would walk by, pause and ask if she was all right. Marlene would nod that she was. Then her face would crumple.

"You want to talk about it? I'm a good listener."

She'd shake her head but start to bawl her eyes out. The man would almost always sit down and try to get her to talk about it.

She had come to town with her husband, Marlene would say. "We drove here from Calgary. He was being so strange the last couple of days. I decided to give him some time on his own."

But, she said, while she was trying on a new dress in a shop, her purse was stolen. Right from under the dressing-room door. Then she returned to the hotel room only to discover that her husband and all of his belongings were gone. There was a note on the pillow: It was over. He'd fallen in love. To add insult to injury, the other woman was her best friend. Marlene's husband had not only checked out, he'd left in the rental car.

"How could he do this to me?"

The usual questions: "Have you tried calling your family?" "Do you have any friends in town?"

Marlene had answers for everything.

"Listen," she'd say. "Is there any way that you—I could wire you the money as soon as I got home." She'd drop her head in her hands and sob.

Maybe it was her acting skills, maybe it was the rich-lady

Chanel suit, but usually she could get two or three hundred dollars out of these marks.

Except this time. In Marlene's third hotel lounge of the day, the guy suggested that she might spend some time with him in his room. "How does a hundred sound?"

———

"Do I look a whore?" Marlene bellowed at me later in our living room. She stood with her hands on hips, staring at me. "A piddling hundred-dollar-hooker?"

I was on the couch. "Why don't you just go back to doing the Birthday Girl?"

"I need a partner for that."

"Call stupid Freddy, then."

"I don't feel like dealing with stupid Freddy's hard-on every time I want to make a few bucks."

"*Gross!* I need to boil my eardrums after that."

"This is a Chanel suit," Marlene pointed out. She had bought it a few months earlier from Freddy. Marlene got some screamin' deals on designer wear from Freddy. "Is there anything about this outfit that says hooker?"

I rolled my eyes. "The guy was a perv. Forget it. *God!*"

She walked to the window. "Should've thrown a horse tranquilizer in his drink and rolled the dumb bastard while he slept." She turned around and stared at me, her face blank. "Some of the girls who buy from Freddy make a pretty good living that way, you know."

"Mom." I shook my head at her. "That's just skeevy."

"What's so skeevy about it? These guys are blowing money on sex, booze, gambling—all kinds of crap. Why shouldn't they pay me for my time? I'm an interesting conversationalist with interesting opinions. It would be a consulting fee."

I stared at her. "What the hell happened to *you can't cheat an honest man?* Until you give him knockout drugs?"

"You think it's *honest* to tell a woman in trouble that you'll help her out if she puts out?"

I just let that one lay there.

A week later, Marlene asked me if I wanted to go to Las Vegas for the weekend.

"I can't. Drew invited me on that youth group thing. Remember? Everyone's going out on sailboats."

Her face went sour. "*Sailboats?* Some Christians. I thought it was easier for a camel to get through the eye of a needle than a rich guy to get into heaven."

"What the hell are you talking about?"

"Listen, kiddo," she said. "They've got Jesus—I need you."

Along with boobs and body hair, I was starting to get a bug up my butt about the kind of hustles that worked best when the mark believed he was doing the right thing. Marlene figured this sudden conscience of mine was the direct result of hanging out with those *holier-than-thou sons-of-bitches* at the church. And maybe it was. I liked those kids. I liked their lives. So I hardly ever came along any more for the hotel games.

————

In the cab from the airport to Caesars Palace, I looked out the window as the last of the sun hit the crummy old neon signs. "It's gross here. They make it look so great on TV."

"Daylight doesn't become it," Marlene said. "It's an inside town. People come here to gamble."

"It's a hole."

In the hotel room, Marlene opened her suitcase on the bed. She took out a pale yellow dress that looked as if it were meant for a large toddler. "Ta-da. Your new frock, madam."

"I'm not wearing that. The hair's bad enough."

"What's wrong with your haircut? It's adorable. You look like Dorothy Hamill."

"*Great.*" I fell back on the bed and stared at the ceiling. "I look like a skating buttercup. I'm *fourteen*. Why can't I just be fourteen?"

"Having an innocent child is part of the illusion. There's nothing innocently childlike about fourteen. Christ, you're impossible lately. If anyone asks, you're twelve. Just throw the dress on, make sure it fits."

Marlene went to the closet, pulled out the ironing board.

I shoved the dress to the side, rolled over and picked around in her open suitcase. There were two little bottles. I pulled one out.

"What's Ketamine? . . . *equivalent to 100mg per ml.*"

"Your *perfume.* There are two little vials in there. I dumped a couple of old perfume samples. We'll refill them with Ketamine."

I read from the bottle. "*Caution: Federal law restricts this drug to use by or on the order of a licensed physician.*"

Going down in the elevator, I checked myself out in the mirrors. The tensor band she had me wear on my chest was killing. It was supposed to squash my little marbles flat and it was tight as hell. "This dress is brutal."

"It's cute." Marlene straightened the collar. "Christ, I think I can still see boobs," she whispered, and mashed a hand down over my chest.

"Mom! Knock it off. I'm totally flat. Jill Williams calls me Reese's Pieces."

Marlene laughed.

"Yeah. Hilarious."

"Just round your shoulders a little."

Marlene led me by the hand through the casino. She sat with me at the nickel slots and ordered Shirley Temples for me. At dinnertime we went to one of the hotel restaurants where the buffet consisted of baron of beef and mountains of crab legs. My mother ordered the buffet. I thought the buffet smelled like vomit-crusted armpit so she ordered me a cheeseburger.

When our food came, Marlene looked me in the eye, poked a finger into an imaginary dimple in her cheek and said, "Lighten up, misery-guts."

I crossed my eyes at her. The tensor band itched and I rubbed my ribs on the table edge, trying to scratch underneath.

So she leaned forward and whispered a rude joke about two skeletons doing it on a tin roof. Cracked me up.

"Gross," I said, coughing on my burger.

Then I remembered this joke that Jill had told at school. Jill and I weren't really friends in those days but I thought she was funny. "Okay," I said, "Little Red Riding Hood is walking through the woods when suddenly the Big Bad Wolf jumps out from behind a tree and he goes, 'Listen, Little Red, I'm going to screw your brains out! So, Little Red reaches into her picnic basket—"

"What do you think of him?" Marlene interrupted. She nodded past me. "The big one."

I looked over my shoulder at two hefty middle-aged guys. Each of them was eating lobster. The bigger one had a thick beard all greasy with guts and butter. Like a grizzly bear eating a giant cockroach. He took one hand off his lobster to wave.

I glanced back at Marlene, who fluttered her hand at him.

"Why the big one?" I whispered.

"He looks greedy," she said, smiling past my shoulder.

Three minutes later, the waitress came to our table. She set some kind of cola in front of me and a boozy thing in front of Marlene. "This is called a 'Beautiful,'" the waitress said. "It's from the gentleman at that table over there. He's wondering if you and your daughter are on your own."

Marlene sighed up at the waitress. "Yes, I guess we are. Oh, maybe you shouldn't tell him that." She mouthed *thank you* over at the grizzly. "Say thank you for your Coke, honey."

I twisted around and waved, giving him a big phony smile.

Grizzly Adams motioned the waitress back to him.

I continued. "Can I finish my joke now? Okay, so, the wolf goes, Red, I'm going to screw your brains out. Then Little Red reaches into her picnic basket, pulls out a gun and says—"

"Excuse me." The waitress was back. "The gentleman would like to know if you would be interested in joining him for a cocktail in the main lounge this evening?"

"Well, I don't know." My mother's face turned pink and she covered her mouth.

You've got to hand it to a chick who can actually blush on cue. I couldn't help but smile as I bit into my burger.

"Nine o'clock?" the waitress said, and Marlene nodded.

———

Marlene and I were in the main lounge before nine.

Marlene spoke softly. "Once it's in, I'll send you to bed and then—"

"Can I go swimming?" I asked out loud. "I brought my bathing suit." I held up the little pink purse she'd given me to carry.

Marlene looked at it as though it were full of turds. "No."

"What's the big deal? Why can't I go swimming?"

Suddenly Marlene's sucker was just a few feet away and I kicked her under the table.

"Who wants to go swimming?" the grizzly said.

Marlene jerked her head up and flashed him a cheery face. "Nobody's going swimming. It's almost her bedtime." She stuck out her hand. "I'm Louise. Thank you *so much* for buying us dinner. That was awfully generous of you."

"Hank." He kissed the back of my mother's hand and took the seat nearest her. "My pleasure. I made out like a bandit at the craps table today. Made a killing!"

"We all had a good day, then. My little one here won twenty-seven dollars at the slots."

"Wow!" He gave me a big dopey smile to show how impressed he was. He glanced from Marlene to me. "Look at the two of you. Can't believe there aren't a hundred men lined up for your company! Let me order us a beverage."

Soon the two of them were gabbing about shows in town. Hank said he had tickets to a late show at some other casino. The show was a little on the risqué side but he'd be happy to spring for a sitter for me.

"I can't stand *sitters*," I said. I was being a bit of a jerk but I had decided that that was my character's attitude for this hustle. Like Sam taught me, it's good to incorporate your real feelings into your character.

Marlene didn't appear to agree with me. Keep it light, keep it simple—that's her motto.

Hank grinned and ordered a second drink.

I took a Rubik's cube out of my purse and started rotating the squares.

"Come on, honey, put that away and be a young lady," Marlene said.

I pouted and stuffed it back in my purse.

"She's okay," Hank said. "What grade are you in, sweetheart?"

"Seven."

"Seven? I thought you'd be in grade 8 for sure. Pretty girl. Boy, if I were twenty years younger!"

I looked at his livery lips and bushy beard. "You're a dirty old man," I said.

"Honey!" Marlene sounded genuinely irate.

Hank laughed his ass off. "That's what they tell me. She's a sharpie, this one."

I rummaged in my purse and took out the Love's Baby Soft perfume vial. I pulled the small plastic plug off and sniffed. It smelled sharp. Like chlorine.

Marlene watched me. Her eyes were nervous, but she sighed and said, "Young ladies don't apply cosmetics at the table, either."

"It's perfume, not cosmetics." I took another whiff.

"Give me that." My mother took the vial and fumbled with the top.

"I'm going to hit the head," Hank announced, and got up and left the table.

"I think you might be overdoing it a little," Marlene whispered once he was out of earshot. She raised her voice and launched into a loud lecture on manners and then, while pushing back the drink glasses, flipped the liquid from the vial into Hank's rye and Coke. "Here's the key. Be a good girl and get ready for bed and I'll be up in a few minutes."

I found the second vial in my purse. It was supposed to be for our next hotel. I held it so that Marlene could see it anyway.

She shook her head. "We're not trying to kill him," she whispered.

I stood as Hank returned. I told him that I was sorry if I'd been rude.

"Rude? Nonsense! We're pals, aren't we? You can be yourself around ol' Hank." He patted my arm. The size and weight of his hand—like a baseball glove—gave me pause for a second. I looked at Marlene.

"I'll be up soon, honey." She kissed my cheek.

I told Hank good night, and made for the elevators.

Sooner or later, this guy was going to try and move Marlene up to his room. She'd put that whole friggin' vial of Ketamine in, though—the goof might just pass out in the bar and then what would she do?

As I waited for the elevator, I looked back toward the lounge. The only way for this to work would be for her to actually go with him to his room. Every hustle we'd ever pulled before this was in public.

The elevator opened and I glanced back again just as Marlene was laughing, her head tipped back. Something about the way her mouth opened, as if she could be screaming, made the hair on my arms prickle.

Don't be a dope, I thought. If anyone can take care of herself, it's her.

Outside our room, I opened my purse for the room key. Inside was my swimsuit, just sitting there in a little ball. I had seen the pool when we checked in that morning. The deck had all this gorgeous marble, and white pillars with Roman statues. I wanted to make like I was Cleopatra taking a dip. Once Marlene was finished with this guy, she'd said she wanted to move to another hotel. I'd never get a chance to swim if I played by her rules.

I looked at my watch. I could go down to the pool for half an hour and she'd never know.

In the lobby, I ducked out of sight and tried to get a look into the lounge. They were gone, near as I could tell. I slipped behind another column. Man, I loved those crazy Roman statues—they were so friggin' cool. Marlene and Hank were definitely not in the lounge any more.

I couldn't wait to step into that warm pool water, the golden lanterns illuminating the deck. I'd be like that chick in the Ban de Soleil commercial. The jingle started up in my head: *Ban de Soleil for the San Tropez tan . . .*

Standing in the lobby, I tried to recall which way the pool was. Everywhere seemed to lead back to the casino. Signs pointed to the elevators, to the shopping area, to the lounge. I headed back across the lobby toward the front desk to ask directions.

As I came closer, I heard one of the receptionists say, "Security will be right up."

I stepped up to the desk.

"Disturbance on the twelfth floor," the receptionist told a man in a black suit on the other side of the counter. "Code two."

My heart started to bang.

The guy in the black suit spoke into a walkie-talkie. "Security to twelve. Code two."

I turned and watched two more suited men rush past me to the lobby elevators.

It can't be her, I thought. She put the whole vial in, didn't she? He was big, though. Maybe one wasn't enough. Why didn't she take the second vial just in case? I looked up at the ceiling as though I could find her that way.

Then I bolted for the elevators.

———

Before the doors opened on the twelfth I could hear the shouting.

I stepped off the elevator and turned toward the noise and there was Marlene on the carpet in the hallway, on all fours, gasping and sobbing. A man and woman were bent over her, trying to help her up, but she would not be touched.

Two men in black suits had Hank pushed face first against the wall, arms twisted behind his back, wrists bent in a way that made them look broken.

Hank howled, his face mashed sideways as he yelled, "It's that bitch, not me. Kick her ass. Fuckin' slut-thief!" There was blood on the white door frame beside him.

I scrambled down the hall. "Leave her alone. Don't touch her!"

Marlene looked up and whispered my name. Blood on her face, she swung her hand, shooing the couple away from her.

"Is this your mother?" the woman asked me. "Sweetheart, maybe you should let us—"

"Fuck off," I said.

The woman shrunk back against her husband. "Somebody should call the police."

"No police." My mother cried it—all her words were cries. I had hold of her now. Her face. Jesus Christ, her beautiful face. Blood ran down from her eyebrow, and from her nose, and rimmed her teeth. She was all broken. Her hands hung in the air in front of her, blood between her fingers.

The yellow dress puffed around me as I knelt on the floor. This never would have happened if Sam were here, I thought. I have to call Sam.

A few feet away, Hank raged and hollered and I hollered right back. "Shut up, you fat prick."

I tried to use the hem of my dress to wipe her hands but the synthetic material wasn't doing the job. "You got any Kleenex?" I asked the woman who still hovered near us.

The woman gave me some tissues and I brought them to Marlene's nose, trying not to hurt her. "We have to go to the hospital," I whispered.

"I want to go home," Marlene whimpered back. "Please."

"I don't think there's a flight tonight."

"Home. Take me home."

"Mom. Please. Maybe we should call Daddy."

"Who? What are you—?" Marlene was panting now. "Take me home."

———

Security seemed just as happy not to call the cops. Eventually I got Marlene back to our room and packed our bags while she sobbed in the bathroom. I got her some ice wrapped in a towel and talked her into lying down for a while. Then I lay in the second double bed and listened to her cry.

It was 4:58 a.m. when Marlene sat up again. "Let's go," she whispered.

I called downstairs and asked to have a taxi waiting.

Lionel Richie and Diana Ross sang "Endless Love" on the radio as we got into the cab. I asked the driver to turn it off, please.

"Leave it," Marlene said.

The desert sun was just coming up and the radio station gave us more Lionel. Tears ran down Marlene's face as "Three Times a Lady" filled the taxi. Richie was in town at some big hotel. We passed his name up in lights.

So much dirt and misery and meanness, and here was Lionel Richie droning away about love two shows a night.

We were on the first flight out of Vegas.

———

It was ten-thirty in the morning by the time we got to Vancouver General. Under her sunglasses, Marlene's face was one big mass of swollen purple bruises and black cuts. She phoned Fat Freddy from a pay phone while we waited in Emergency. She cried. She whispered bits and pieces of what had happened to her.

When a doctor finally saw us, she told him that she'd fallen down the stairs. It was her divorce, she said. The stress was giving her insomnia and the lack of sleep was making her clumsy.

They put five stitches in her eyebrow and taped her nose, gave her prescriptions for Percocet for pain and some Ativan to calm her nerves. Freddy picked us up and drove us back to the apartment.

On the way home, he asked Marlene how much Ketamine she'd used. "A hundred milligrams," she told him. "One millilitre dumped into his drink. You said—"

"Orally? Ah, honey, no." He reached for her hand. "Hundred by injection, sure. Orally—that'd barely put a German shepherd to sleep."

He murmured sympathy and kissed her hand as he drove. I stared at the back of his head.

———

For weeks, Marlene wouldn't go out. She stared at the TV and popped painkillers and Ativan. She started sipping vodka and milk sometime around noon each day.

When the phone would ring, she barely looked at me. "Tell them I'm not home." Unless it was Freddy. Suddenly Freddy was the only one who could really understand what had happened to her.

He came by the apartment to see her every couple of days. He brought her a Hummel figurine the first week: a little blonde girl bathing a baby. Marlene touched the smooth, pale arms on the little girl and tears rolled down her face.

Freddy smiled. "Cute, isn't it? I thought you'd like it."

"I'm a terrible mother," Marlene sobbed. She cried full-on for a good ten minutes.

I went into my room and closed the door.

Whenever Freddy made a pest of himself after that, he came bearing designer blouses instead.

It was two weeks after Vegas that I came in from school and Freddy was there, joining her in a drink. This time he had brought her a box of European chocolates.

"Good thing you girls started collecting that welfare cheque a few years back," he said. "That welfare's a nice little safety net for a single gal."

I could feel myself stiffen. "We don't *need* welfare. It's just available, that's all."

"Looks like you need it *now*, sweetheart," Freddy said. "I think you definitely need it now." He seemed to leer when he said it.

I wondered whether it was the government cheques or the vulnerability of Marlene's half-broke face that turned him on.

FIVE

IN SOME SOCIAL worker's office, Ruby, Jill and I each sit in one of those moulded plastic chairs. Lou dropped us off. He had to get some gas, he said. He'd just wait in the parking lot for us. Who could blame him? What normal person would want to visit the Department of Child Welfare?

We've been here maybe ten minutes and we haven't said a thing. All you can hear is the turning of pages. Ruby is reading a pamphlet on fetal alcohol syndrome and Jill is flipping through an issue of *People* she brought with her. I'm staring at the floor thinking, where the fuck is my dad anyway? Everyone wants to blame Marlene but, really, if you think about it, this whole thing is Sam's fault. If he hadn't screwed up, he wouldn't have landed in jail and he and Marlene never would have split up. And if my parents hadn't split up, we wouldn't have been so broke and if we hadn't been broke, Marlene never would have tried the

46

bullshit hustle that sent her off the rails in the first place. That's the origin of the problem. That's the forensic explanation.

The door opens and Jill and Ruby put their reading down. The social worker says hello and introduces herself. I don't hear her name.

She sits down and sets a file on her desk. The tab says *Bell*. Our family file. It's thicker than I would have thought. What the hell could they have in there? Marlene and I have probably been on their radar for six years now. That's what happens when you go on welfare. Tabs.

I stare at that file while the social worker asks me what's been going on at home. I guess I don't answer the first time she asks, because she repeats it clearly. Everything is quiet for another few seconds. I feel like a stuffed animal. White cotton in my eyes and mouth, clogging my whole skull, spilling out of me. I can't remember how to talk. If I could make words right now, I'd say, *Who are you again? And who am I?*

I glance at Ruby and Jill.

"Go ahead, Sammie," Ruby says. "Tell her what's been happening at home."

I'm floating in white, white clouds. Nothing but white, white noise.

Someone needs to bang me on the side of the head, the way you do with a TV that's on the fritz.

"Samantha," the social worker says, her tone stern. "Can you tell me what's going on with your mother, Marlene?"

Marlene's name is a rap in the mouth. Marlene. Marlene's in big trouble. Me too.

"She wants to kill herself . . ." Should I say about the drinking? Ruby will tell anyway. Big mouth. "She's drinking. She's very . . . um . . . she's sad right now. Depressed. For the last few months, she can't even . . . I write out the cheques for the bills and the rent and—" I curl one hand into a writing position, then cradle it in my other hand to illustrate. "I hold her hand on the pen so she can sign."

My fake Marlene signatures flash to mind and my head aches. They can see it all, the film of my sick thoughts projected on the wall behind me. I am the dirty floor. I am the filthy dishes. No one says *Poor Marlene.*

The social worker asks about my father. Samuel Bell, she says. Is that correct? Where is he?

"I don't know."

The day after I got to Jill's place, I had called Sam again and given him the phone number. He said, "So, you got a place to stay. That's good. Okey-doke. Real good. I can't stay on the phone, cuz I'm drivin' to Montreal this afternoon for a game. I'll give you a buzz in the next couple days."

I'm not telling this chick anything. He'll call. Eventually.

The social worker makes a note.

Ruby begins to talk now about her and Lou, their former status as group home operators. The department is well acquainted with them, Ruby says, and their work with *disadvantaged youth.* They decided to close down their home five years ago, but under the circumstances they would like to take Sammie in.

Her. She. Sammie. I'm like the stray dog in the room. The

mongrel. Someone should put me to sleep and be done with it.

Sammie's mother is in desperate need of a wake-up call, Ruby says. Ruby suggests that the department appoint Ruby and Lou as temporary guardians and begin sending support cheques for Sammie to them. They could deduct the amount from Marlene's welfare.

Is she fucking *serious?* How is Marlene supposed to live? She couldn't run a decent hustle on a retarded priest these days.

"No."

All eyes turn to me, the talking dog. "She's barely making it as it is," I whisper.

The social worker eyes me. She must see a thousand jerks like me every week. She must wash her hands all day.

"I'm inclined to leave Mrs. Bell's support as it is. The red tape involved to adjust support—We can appoint you guardians for short-term placement. That sounds prudent. And we'll just send an additional cheque for Samantha while she's with you. For a maximum of three months, at which point we can re-evaluate the situation."

Ruby's mouth tightens. She makes a cranky growling noise. "Why should that woman receive financial support for a child she can't take care of? Seems like rewarding bad behaviour, if you ask me."

Jesus. What's it to her?

"That's not fair," I mutter.

"It's not fair at all," Ruby says.

"I'll take it under advisement." The social worker's lips blow out as she exhales. She gives a curt nod to Ruby and says,

"You can pick up the cheque here on Monday or we can mail it to you if you prefer."

She hands me her card and tells me to contact her anytime if I should feel the need to talk. She wishes us good luck.

I could punch Ruby in her tubby little kisser right now.

SIX

SOMETIMES I WISH Marlene did still hold a torch for Sam. She could probably get him back if she wanted to. We could all have each other back. But she doesn't. That's not to say she didn't love him at one time. He loved her too—I know he did. The Lady Leni, my dad used to call her. He called her Leni when he loved her, short for Marlene. I was little then. We were all little, in my head.

"If you went bald, I'd shine your head every day," my dad once said to her.

"That's beautiful," Marlene said. "*I'd die without you, Leni,*" she said, acting out what should have been his part. "*I'm yours till the end of time.*"

Sam grinned and went back to marking cards. This was early on, before he was a real card mechanic. Later, he could stack himself a nice cooler, slip the fixed deck back into a poker game without anyone having a clue. A true mechanic doesn't need to mark any cards. He can stack the deck just so and deal what he wants to who he wants and nobody's the wiser.

Sam raised the tip of the marker from the flip side of the card, squinted at his craftsmanship. "I never left nobody in my life," he said and set the card aside to dry.

My mother told me about this conversation some time ago. The way I figure it, she and Sam must have been nuts about each other at one point or why would she have worked so hard to piss him off?

We were living in Toronto when Marlene split on me the first time. She had buggered off on Sam before, but never me.

It was August. The air in Toronto was muggy and hot. We'd left Vancouver in June and Marlene wanted to go back. She often dropped her head to wave a hand or magazine at her sweaty neck. "It's like living under a dog's tongue," she'd say. Then she'd get all soppy about the Pacific, the pure sweet breeze of it, how gorgeous the hydrangeas would be—fat blue heads, big as basketballs. Not like these anemic little nothings that grew in Toronto. Hydrangeas seemed to be the symbol of all that was bad in Toronto and good in Vancouver.

The real problem was that Sam didn't take her out with him any more. Not that my mother and father had ever worked together all that much. Sam's forte was card sharping and Marlene didn't play cards. But Sam stopped bringing her along altogether when we moved east. He said it was because they didn't have a free sitter for me the way we used to in Vancouver. Back on Willow Street, I liked to sleep over next door with

Abby Elliot and her big sister Joy, so my parents were all set. Once in a while, Sam would bring Mrs. Elliot a present—say a cashmere sweater or a Royal Doulton figurine. If Mrs. Elliot knew the stuff was hot, she never let on.

No Mrs. Elliot in Toronto, though. And Sam said we had to keep the nut down—he wasn't going to work all night paying for a bloody babysitter.

Working all night was the other significant issue. The first time it happened in Toronto, Marlene was bug-eyed furious. He came home the next morning to a wife with sharp fists and a thousand teeth. My father wasn't big on yelling. He closed the kitchen door as they argued. I crept into the dining room to listen.

"What do you think I was doin' all night?" I could hear Sam's playful chuckle. Out all night, but his shirt was still smooth. As if he'd ironed it just before driving home.

"They had no telephone?" It was the second time Marlene had asked this, and so she hollered to make sure he heard. "You couldn't use a pay phone?"

"I didn't have any slugs on me."

"If you weren't such a liar I'd say you were the cheapest prick I've ever known."

"I had a game," Sam told her again.

"Did Peggy happen to be at this game?"

"Peggy don't play cards," he told her. Peggy was kind of a family friend, a booster they knew. "Games go all night lotta times. You know that."

"You had a game, all right. See how you like it." I heard the zip of her purse and I rushed back to the living room.

The kitchen door flung open just as I made it into the armchair.

"Leni," he called as she stormed over to where I was balled up in front of the TV.

I was supposed to start grade 3 in two weeks and already I missed the summer.

"I'm going out for a while, honey," she said.

"Are you bringing me?" I didn't want to stay with Sam if he was in trouble. Didn't want it rubbing off.

"Daddy'll make you lunch." She smoothed the hair out of my eyes. Her fingertips were like feathers.

Marlene kissed my temple with loud lips, moved her nose to my hair and breathed deep. Standing up, she winked at me, her face stiff, as though she might break into a million pieces.

She threw open the front door so hard it slammed the wall. I remember the way the sunrays burst around her dark silhouette as she paused, looking into the light. It made me think of that song that kept playing on the radio, "Knockin' on Heaven's Door." She walked down the steps as if she'd be back any second, leaving the door open behind her.

By eight o'clock that night, Marlene still wasn't home. Sam heated up wieners and beans from a can. The first spoonful made me gag. He looked at his watch and tossed me a banana. Got to go to work, he said. My father's front was that he was an agent for First Rate Real Estate. He had business cards that said so, and once, while we were driving, he pointed out a For Sale sign on a front lawn that listed Sam Bell as the realtor. He'd only sold one house, so far as I knew.

"I got to sell some houses tonight, okay?" His voice was singsong dopey, as if I was barely out of diapers. As if I had no idea. "He thinks kids are stupid," Marlene once told me. "He thinks they're deaf, dumb and blind."

Suddenly he produced a chocolate Easter bunny still in the box. The rabbit was warped and nearly flat, as if Sam had forgotten it on the roof all summer. "Don't answer the door for anyone," he warned me.

After he'd gone, I curled up on the couch in front of a movie-of-the-week called *Trilogy of Terror* and ate the rabbit with a carton of milk.

My father phoned sometime around ten. "What's doin'?"

I stared at the TV as a come-to-life Zuni doll chased cross-eyed Karen Black around her apartment with a spear. "Bring me home some Kentucky Fried Chicken?"

"In a while," he said. "I got four more houses to sell."

It must have been midnight when he called back and woke me. Now there was a western on television.

"How come you took so long to answer?" he asked me. "You okay there?"

He said he'd be home to tuck me in soon, just two more houses. I hung up the phone and stared at the TV. Did he think I'd shoot off my mouth if he talked straight with me? Was he showing off for someone in the room with him?

When the front door finally opened, yellow sunlight was streaming through the windows. Heels clacked on hardwood.

"What are you doing on the couch?" Marlene asked. She looked like she hadn't slept. "Where's your father?"

I shrugged. "He had to work."

Her mouth opened but nothing came out at first. Finally she said, "All night? Are you saying that he was out *all night?*"

I sucked in my lips and kept quiet.

She stomped upstairs. I followed, watching her go from room to room. She hauled out a suitcase, threw it on my bed and chucked in clothing from my drawers. She had just put a pile of her own stuff in when the front door slammed. Marlene tossed a sweater at me and told me to get my shoes on.

Suitcase in one hand and my arm in the other, she shoved past Sam on the stairs. "You left your kid by herself all night. You *puke.*"

He looked to me, his eyes pleading. "Why'd you stop answerin' that phone?"

"I fell asleep," I said, my eyes down. No one wants to be on the losing team.

———

"We're going to stop in and visit Mel," Marlene informed me after she gave the taxi driver an address on College Street.

"Who's Mel?" I asked, staring back at our house as the cab pulled away.

"My friend," she said. "I should have taken you with me yesterday to meet him. You'll like Mel. I bet you two will get along like a house on fire."

Mel and his buddy Rick were sitting on Mel's front porch in lawn chairs, drinking and watching the traffic on College Street, trolley cars clanging back and forth. When Marlene and I stepped out of the taxi, the cool smirk slid off Mel's face. His jaw clenched at the sight of our suitcase.

"Miss me?" my mother called to him in a smooth, light voice, the one she used when she really wanted something. "We were on our way to a hotel," she said as we climbed the stairs. "Thought we'd drop in."

The house looked a little beat-up, the way a place does when everyone's moved out and you're the last one left.

Mel's pal Rick stood up, grinning. They both stank of rum-and-Coke. "Hotel? Why don't you stay with us and loan the place a little class."

Mel shot him a look.

I kicked the word *class* around in my head. *Classy.* Marlene Bell was *classy*, I thought. The Lady Leni, Sam called her, and she did look like someone you might see come feet first out of a limousine, followed by long legs and a sleek dress. Mel and Rick were more like the guys who call at you from a carnival booth.

Rick rubbed his hands on his jeans and stepped forward to take our suitcase. He was lanky with pinched, ropy muscles. He wore flares and a black tank top.

Mel grunted as he pushed himself out of the chair. He put a hand on my mother's elbow and kissed her cheek. His mouth tugged to one side when he looked at me.

Back in Vancouver, Amy Elliot's big sister, Joy, used to refer to old guys who thought they were groovy as dinks. "Man, what a dink," she said when she spotted fat old Elvis squeezed into his jumpsuit on TV. Mel was a super-dink, from my perspective,

swaggering around in a slippery shirt, three buttons undone
and a gold cross dangling. He wore a brown leather blazer
though the city felt like a tropical terrarium.

As the rum flowed that night, the mood lightened. Out on the
front porch, Mel sprawled in his lawn chair, one hand clutching
the glass on his knee, the other draped across Marlene's shoulders. My mother perched next to him on a kitchen chair and
matched him nearly drink for drink.

———

Later that night, I lay in a spare room that seemed to be Mel's
storage closet. His house was cluttered with full ashtrays and
thumby, scratched records. There were busted appliances here
and there, each one with its guts hanging out, as if he had tried
to fix it with no idea how to put it back together. Aside from
the single bed against the wall, the spare room was a home for
banged-up packing boxes, some filled with stacks of old *Pent-
house* magazines and others with little kids' stuff: a baby chair,
a toy xylophone, a plastic baseball bat, trains and little cars. A
mountain of rumpled women's clothes spilled out of the closet.

Eventually Marlene came in and curled up beside me on the
bed. There were no blankets or sheets, just a sleeping bag.

"How long are we going to stay here?" I whispered.

"Until your daddy learns his lesson," she told me. "We're
having an adventure!" She blew a raspberry into my shoulder
and the smell of rum wafted.

When I woke again she was gone. Low moans mixed with

shushing came from the room next door. I thought of Sam in his and Marlene's bed. I imagined my father lying in the same position I was, thinking of me at exactly the same moment.

———

On day two at Mel's, I became the official gofer.

Mel might say, "Where the hell are my matches," which would immediately be followed by, "Hey, Suzie Q!" That was me.

They paid me in leftover change to run down to the corner store. I didn't like the way Mel called me Suzie Q, or the way he said, *Heavy!* all the time and, *Can you dig it?* like a dink-and-a-half. But being the gofer was something to do and there was dough to be made.

Late that afternoon, just after a third cola run, my father pulled up in front of Mel's house. He got out of his spotless Cadillac and called up to the porch. A passing streetcar clanged through his words.

My mouth hung. I wondered if Sam had just happened to drive by and spot us or if he'd done some detective work.

Mel and Rick stared down from their lawn chairs. Perched between them, Marlene straightened, peering hard like a snake about to strike.

Sam came around the nose of his car and stepped up onto the sidewalk.

"I thought I told you to go ahead and fuck yourself, Sam the Man," Marlene sang down the steps as if it were all a game. She folded her arms and gave him the smuggest look she had.

Mel took a drag off his smoke. Skinny Rick set his rum-and-Coke down on the porch and stood. He wore a translucent purple shirt. I caught sight of his nipples and felt bad for it.

"I want my kid," Sam said. His lips were thin and hard. He looked rich in his starched yellow shirt and smooth slacks. *Classy.*

My guts zipped as Sam came toward the steps.

Rick moved to the edge of the porch, staring down as my father made his way up. Just as Sam veered in my direction, Rick's hand shot out and he shoved my dad.

Sam stumbled back, arms pinwheeling. My bare feet dug at the porch as he lurched backward to the pavement. But he didn't fall—somehow he got his feet under him.

Once he'd caught his balance, Sam looked from Rick to his Lady Leni. I didn't turn my head but I knew Marlene was grinning. Sam's eyes never once met mine.

Look at me, I thought. *Take me, take me, take me.*

"I'll be back," he said, his voice high and tight. He turned and walked back to his car, climbed in.

Rick's hands twitched as if he'd been gypped somehow.

"That was heavy," Mel said, exhaling.

"Thank you, *Rick,*" Marlene said.

I stared after Sam's disappearing Cadillac.

———

The next afternoon, the mood on the porch was sulky. I offered the same gofer services, but refused to hand anything over until whoever had done the hiring paid up. Mel had stiffed me twenty-five cents the day before.

"Knock it off, kid," Marlene snarked. "You sound like your old man. Big Man Short-shit." Her eyelids were thick and her enunciation had gone sloppy.

Mel kept his eyes trained on the sidewalk, and Marlene followed his gaze to two long-haired girls: teenagers in faded denim shorts and kerchief blouses. Mel and Rick were mute as four long, thin legs scissored past.

Marlene snorted. "Could they yank those shorts any higher up their cracks?"

Mel shifted in his chair. A minute later, he announced that he was heading to the store to get his own smokes. He could use the exercise, he said.

"See if I care," I muttered.

Rick drummed fingers on the arm of his lawn chair.

I moped on the top step and watched the streetcars pass while my mother squinted down the block. Mel stopped on the corner and wangled his way into a conversation with those two long-haired girls.

"Sammie," my mother hissed. "Go down there to where Mel is and say, 'Daddy, Mommy wants you to come home now.'"

I picked at some dry skin on my foot. "No."

"Don't be such a spoilsport. Come on. I'll give you fifty—I'll give you seventy-five cents. '*Daddy, Mommy wants you to come home now.*'"

I held out an open palm in her direction. Three quarters later, I trudged down the porch steps.

The girls stood close to one another, arms crossed. Kerchief blouses floated in the traffic heat. Feet set wide like a cowboy, Mel kept one hand on his belt and gestured with his cigarette as he gabbed.

When I reached them, I paused, trying to get up the guts.

Mel eyed me. I stared down at the sidewalk and mumbled my line.

Glancing at her friend, the bonier girl said, "We better get going."

"She's not my kid." Mel smiled at them. "Her old lady just got dumped. You know how it is." He gave them a wink.

"My boyfriend gets really pissed off when I'm late," the girl explained.

"He's mental-jealous," the other one added. She smirked and tugged the bony one by the belt loop and they walked away.

"Come by for a drink sometime," Mel called after them.

Shoulders hunched, the girls giggled their way down the sidewalk.

Mel snatched an angry drag off his smoke and headed off toward the store. He didn't turn his head when he said, "Tell your mother to call her old man."

I headed back to the house, hopping on the hot pavement.

Marlene was now sitting halfway down Mel's steps. Rick had disappeared. My mother's face moved from stony to something like pity as she touched a dry leaf on the sickly hydrangea bush beside her.

———

I still wonder how Sam found us that day. He's like that, though. He knows things.

That's why I know he'll come looking for me now too. He came that time and he'll come this time. Because I'm his kid. *I want my kid.* I bet he's thinking that right now.

It's hard for him because he works a lot. And he has to travel for work. He's just really busy. He owns two buildings in Toronto. Probably others that I don't even know about. All that and he's never had a joe job in his life. That's my dad for you. He doesn't talk, he *acts.*

He hasn't called me back yet but he will. I'm his kid.

SEVEN

LIGHT SHINES THROUGH slits in the wine-coloured lace curtain on Jill's high little basement window. I just dreamed that I was on a trapeze in the circus and Drew was on another one. We kept swinging back and forth. There was no net under us, just a huge bonfire. We weren't scared, though. We were holding hands and the fire was part of our act. I couldn't stop smiling.

Kind of disappointing to wake up here in the basement with Jill. It's summer vacation, though, which means I don't have to do *anything*.

She's still sleeping hard. I never saw anyone sleep like Jill. Her arms lie above her shoulders, framing her face, as if she's posing for *Playboy*. The first time I saw her do that, I thought she was faking—trying to look sexy. She was out cold, though. I guess some people are just naturally glamorous types.

She doesn't wake up when I get out of bed, so I leave her there.

Upstairs, in the kitchen, Ruby is making pancakes. The house is thick with the smell of bacon fat. I can't remember the last time I saw pancakes in the morning. And we almost never have bacon at home. Marlene thinks bacon's a rip-off. *They charge you through the nose for a pound of pork fat,* she says. Sam never cared about stuff like that. When you go grocery shopping with Sam, you can throw whatever the hell you like in the cart: bacon, big thick steaks, fancy cheeses with French names, Coke and 7UP (the real stuff, not the store-brand crap), and genuine maple syrup. We used to have a total ball in the supermarket.

Jill's dad is at the table. He props his two giant forearms on either side of his plate, and he lowers his bearded face to take a bite off the bacon slice in his right hand. A regular lumber-jack. Lou's like Paul Bunyan. Everything looks miniature when he's nearby. He lowers his head to his fork and takes a mouthful of pancake. A little syrup dribbles into the fur around his lips.

"How are you this fine morning, Samantha?" he says, sitting upright when he notices me.

Lou is kind of formal. At least with me. So polite I figure he's joking half the time.

"Ducky," I say, and sit across from him.

When he smiles, the balls of his cheeks squish right up under his eyes. I try to picture Lou at Oakalla Prison ordering crimi-nals around, rapping his club against iron bars, telling them to shut their damn traps. He must have a desk job.

Lou's got thick, dark, wavy hair. Like Jill's. I glance at Ruby's short steely curls. Marlene would die before she'd let her hair go grey while a guy like Lou sat at her table. She'd sooner go bald.

If you went bald, I'd shine your head every day.

The phone rings.

Ruby gets up and starts toward the hall off the kitchen but the ringing stops. She keeps going. In the hall, I hear her open the door down to the basement. "You got that, Jill?" she says.

My name is croaked up from the basement as if from the bottom of a swamp.

Ruby steps back into the kitchen. "Sammie, phone's for you."

I get up slowly. What if it's Drew on the other end? I dreamed about him. So it seems like it must be him. I bet Marlene gave him the number here. Now I'm going to get my head chewed off for going AWOL. I don't blame him. I'm a shitty friend these days. I really am.

Rubbing my hands on my pyjama pants, I try to remember the details of the Drew dream before I pick the receiver up off the hall table. People always like it when you dream about them.

"It's me," my mother says. Her voice could cut through bone. "I suppose you've got it pretty good over there."

I stare at the wall. There's a little notepad in front of me, with a pencil dangling by a string:

Jill—Crystal called.

Mom—Adele called.

"Were you planning to come home at *some* point and do this laundry or what?"

"Um." That's all I say. From behind me I hear the slow thump of Jill coming up the basement steps.

"What about the dishes? Are you ever going to do *anything* around here?"

"Yeah, I—um." I glance over my shoulder as Jill reaches the hallway. Eyes squinty, she trudges into the bathroom and shuts the door.

"Jesus Christ, Samantha." Marlene almost never calls me Samantha.

"I'll come over. In around an hour?"

"Fine," she says, and the line goes dead.

Standing in the hallway, I forget which door I was about to go through. I turn toward the basement. I should get dressed.

"Sammie?" Ruby calls.

I come back to the kitchen entrance. "My mom. I just have to go home for a bit. There's a bunch of laundry."

Jill steps out of the bathroom and through a yawn says, "What's going on?" Ruby exchanges a glance with Lou, who doesn't look at me, just grabs another pancake and mops up the syrup on his plate.

"Call her back and tell her you're not coming," Ruby says.

"I just have to do—"

"You don't have to do anything. Marlene has to clean up her own mess."

I don't like the way Ruby says *Marlene,* like it's a swear word or something.

Jill is right behind me. I can smell her Opium perfume. Her old boyfriend Roman bought her that. (I'd bet anything he got it hot.) Everything Jill owns is choking with that musky Opium smell. Enough to make you *boke,* as she would say.

I move to the side and let her pass. She just stands there, though, tightens the belt of her fuzzy purple bathrobe and says, "Mom's right."

My face is heating up. "Some of it's mine too. The laundry . . ."

"That's fine," Ruby says.

"I can help her out if I want."

"You'd be doing her a bigger favour if you said no," Ruby says.

I bite a hangnail and look at Jill's fuzzy bathrobe. I wish I could curl up in mountains of purple plush right now.

"Call her back and tell her you're not coming," Ruby says again, trying to keep eye contact with me.

I turn back into the hall and look at the phone. I pick up the receiver. There's a spot of blood where the hangnail used to be and I suck at it, trying to remember my own number.

After a few seconds I take my finger from my mouth and use it to dial.

When Marlene answers, I stutter and stumble on every word. "Hi, um, yeah, I—I'm not coming over."

There's a pause at her end. Then she says, "What do you *mean,* Mommy?" Marlene's voice has turned high and small, as if she's playing a part. A kid in a scary movie. "When *are* you coming home, Mommy? There's no food. And you have to do laundry."

"What's wrong with you?" I whisper.

"I'm *scared,* Mommy," she says.

The base of the phone is mounted on the wall. I tug the knotted phone cord and pull the receiver with me into the bathroom.

"Why are you calling me *Mommy?*"

"Because you're my mommy!" she whispers back.

"If I'm Mommy, then who are you supposed to be?"

"I'm Sammie!" Marlene says.

"What are you *doing?*"

"I'm playing games." Marlene sounds *really* creepy now.

I attempt to close the bathroom door but the cord is too short.

"Oh yeah?" I try to keep my voice low and steady the way they say you should with mad dogs and crazy people. "I'm not playing with *you*. And I'm not coming over there."

Silence.

"Okay?"

"Fine," she says, all clipped and pissy. The line goes dead again.

I hang up.

In the kitchen, all female eyes are watching me. Lou picks up his mug and stares into it as if he's reading tea leaves.

I sit at the table. Jill does too.

Lou pushes his chair back and announces that he's going out to the backyard to work on the broken part of the fence.

When the back door closes behind him, Ruby says, "How are you doing, Sammie?"

"Fine."

"Good. Good girl." She looks out the window, and watches her husband cross the backyard. He kicks at the loose board on the fence, and she says, "I think I might go visit Adele today," breezy as you please. Just like nothing happened.

Ruby and Jill make small talk about this Adele chick and how ancient she is, five hundred years old and still kicking. Their voices are hyper-cheerful.

I look down at the two pancakes on my plate and decide to throw some bacon on top. I reach for the bottle of pancake syrup, stare for a second at Aunt Jemima's grinning face, that kerchief wrapped around her head as if she just escaped from *Gone with the Wind*.

Corn syrup. That's all it is. Fake. Plastic bottle with lousy corn syrup and food colouring. Ruby thinks she's so much better than us and she can't even buy real maple syrup.

I flip the cap and squirt it all over my pancakes and bacon and then chew and chew, trying to get full.

EIGHT

AS I WALK down Kingsway, the traffic roars by and gives me a bit of relief, drowns me out. Kingsway is the main road that cuts through Burnaby. Kingsway feels like a strip mall that goes on forever.

While I was eating those crappy corn-syrup pancakes, Jill asked me if I wanted to go with her to meet Crystal Norris at The Pantry. *Pass.* Although Crystal hasn't shoulder-checked me lately. Since she discovered that Jill and I are friends she tolerates me pretty well.

Don't care, though. Don't feel like talking. Don't feel like being tolerated.

Anonymity. That's what I want.

How can I stay in that house? Every day, they know more and more. Both of them yap-yap-yapping and listening to my conversations and telling me what to do.

I don't know if Marlene's just being a brat or if she's actually gone crazy. At the end of that call, she didn't sound crazy. She sounded pissed off.

What the fuck is she *doing?* I don't get it. And where the hell is Sam? What if he called Jill's house and they never told me? Maybe they forgot to write it down on the little pad on the wall. I wonder if I should just phone him again. Just to say hi. That's what a normal daughter would do.

I need to think. I need to feel air in my hair. I wish I could be in a convertible, by the ocean, downtown at English Bay. A person like me should live downtown.

I keep walking west on Kingsway in the direction of downtown Vancouver. It's only about seven or eight miles from here. Man, I'd like to move back to town. Marlene says I'm an urban snob. Fact is we were both die-hard urbanites before Sam buggered off, and even then, for the first couple of years at least, we managed to stay in the city. Until all that shit happened. One bad hustle pretty much turned Marlene off The Life for good. Mostly it was welfare after that. And moving farther and farther east every year, to cheaper and cheaper places, until we were smack in the middle of Burnaby. The Burbs.

Burnaby used to have one thing going for it—I was closer to Drew. But now I can't bear to look him in the eye. Not after everything he's seen. He sure as hell didn't need to know about Marlene and me. I should never have phoned him that night; I should have kept him pure and separate from our bullshit.

But it was getting so I started to really panic when Marlene didn't come home till late. Once upon a time, she used to leave me notes. Then that whole note thing went out the window. Meanwhile, if I'd ever disappeared and didn't call or leave a note to say where I was, she would've *peaked!* It felt like the only thing worse than Marlene being home was waiting for Marlene to come home. Three nights before I left, I got so freaked out, I wrapped my arms around my knees and sat there on the couch, squeezing and rocking back and forth like some mental patient. What if she got hurt, who'd call me? I got so riled I actually found Fat Freddy's number and phoned him.

I had to go into Marlene's file box for his number. Marlene has a small plastic file box with alphabetized index cards that detail every bar she ever hit with the Birthday Girl and a few other scams. She used to be very systematic. She wrote down the town, the bar, the bartender, the jewellery involved and who she was with at the time. This stuff dates back to when Sam was around. Freddy's card has his phone number and any leads that are specific to Freddy. The details are coded. I don't think a cop would ever know what he was reading.

"Heya, kid," said Freddy when he picked up. "Na, I haven't seen your mother lately. I figured she was either workin' solo or lambin' it. Ha ha . . ." That's Fat Freddy for you, like some prehistoric creature from the late, late show. My dad kind of talks like that too. Sam calls crooked guys "rounders" and regular guys "square johns." I was pretty old before I realized most people don't talk that way.

"You all alone over there, Sammie?"

"My boyfriend's here," I lied.

"Uh-oh! I won't tell if you don't!"

Talking to Freddy only made me more paranoid.

I hung up. But I couldn't shake that black-cloud kind of feeling. I got out the White Pages and flipped chunks of grey leaves. It was almost nine o'clock now.

I started by phoning hospitals to see if she'd ended up in the emergency ward: Burnaby General, Vancouver General, St. Paul's. It wasn't as if Marlene had never had a wreck in the past. She'd totalled that old Nova of hers last year.

When the hospitals didn't have her, I wondered if she'd be stupid enough to get drunk and try to work. Marlene's not the kind of girl to learn from her mistakes. And what if she got busted? Who'd call me?

I phoned the main police station downtown. When they answered, I hung up. People like us don't call cops.

Then I panicked some more.

There are perfectly legit reasons to call the cops, I told myself. Normal people call the cops all the time.

I phoned back. I asked if anyone had come across a woman called Marlene Bell.

The cop laughed. "No. Should we be expecting her?"

"She's—She should be home and I thought . . . an accident, maybe."

Silence on his end, and then, "Okay, why don't I call you back if I hear anything? Who knows, eh?"

I couldn't hang up now. That'd be suspicious. What if he traced the call?

Normal people phone the police.

I told him my number.

An hour later he called back. They had Marlene.

I asked if she was okay. "Will she lose her driver's licence?"

"She wasn't driving. We found her wandering around Broadway and Main. If you want to come get her—actually, we'll hang on to her for a couple more hours, let her sober up. Come after midnight. You driving?"

"I don't have my licence yet," I mumbled. "I just turned sixteen."

His silence was the worst part. "Do you have someone you can call?" he finally asked. "And bring her some clothes."

"Clothes?"

"She was wearing a sleeping bag and one clog when we picked her up. Come by anytime after midnight." He rattled off the address.

Who do you call when your mother's in jail? How totally screwed is that?

Who did I have? My dad? No. Fat Freddy? Forget it. Who? Drew. I had Drew. Drew was the only one in the world who really gave a shit.

I called his house and his mother answered. "It's ten-thirty at night, Samantha." Her voice was suspicious and tinny.

Drew's mother had my number all right. Drew told me once that she'd said I was a bad apple.

She called her son and told him to be quick about it.

I kept swallowing and looking at the clock. After midnight, the cop had said. How could Drew help me after midnight?

And if he did help me then he'd know. He'd know who I was and what kind of people I come from. For real.

———

Drew pulled up in his dad's car at five to one. He had told me he'd be there at quarter past twelve. "What took you so long?"

"You think he just handed me the keys? My dad'll shit a brick if he catches me."

"Sorry."

He glanced down at my hands. "What's in the bag?"

"Nothing." I scrunched the plastic in my lap. "Clothes. Can we go?"

Drew carefully put the car into drive. Streetlights illuminated the hard, red bumps on his skin, turning them purple in the night. He was so embarrassed about his zits. In this light they made him look wounded. I wished we could be quiet and hug for a long time. But we didn't do that sort of thing. Drew and I aren't touchy types. So, instead, we eased forward, Drew's hands firmly at ten and two o'clock on the wheel.

As we got closer to the station, the streets got grimier and lonelier—as if the whole neighbourhood was a place that served you right for being a screw-up. It was past one-thirty when we parked in front of the station, a big, ugly brick building with small, caged windows lit yellow. Drew turned off the ignition.

"I can't do this," I blurted.

He looked at me. "You want me to go? I'll go."

I nodded and handed him the bag of clothes. He handed me the car key. "In case you want to listen to the radio or something." He got out.

He blinked up at the police station a moment. I watched his skinny legs as he climbed the concrete steps.

Once he disappeared through the doors, I stared at the dashboard and listened to the engine click as it cooled.

"*I'll kill you!*" someone yelled. I twisted around to see two guys staggering down the block. One guy threw a fist into the other's chest and sent him sprawling. These two assholes were loose and Marlene was behind bars. In the movies, they always make it look all adorable when some chick is drunk off her butt. But in real life, people hate her—they want to make her disappear.

I clicked the lock down on my door.

Eventually Drew and my mom pushed through the front doors, Drew with a red-plaid sleeping bag under one arm and his opposite hand under my mother's elbow. Marlene pulled free, leaned on the banister and slid the rest of the way down the stairs. She stumbled off the last step and Drew caught her elbow again.

Giggling, she said, "You are my prince," and grabbed Drew's face.

"Shut up," I said to the dashboard.

"God, you're *cute!*" she yelled at him.

Drew kept a hand across her back and brought her over to the passenger side. I shoved my door open. Marlene's face lit up when I got out.

Then, reading my eyes, she said, "Oops. I'm in trouble. My little girl thinks I'm a *loo-hoo-hooser.*" She made an *L* out of her thumb and finger and planted it on her forehead.

I handed Drew the keys and got into the back. I wanted her up front, not sitting behind me, playing with my hair or trying to maul me. I watched Marlene watching Drew as he closed the passenger door and I wished we had put her in the trunk.

As he walked around to the driver's side, Marlene turned around in her seat and looked at me. "He's a *doll*," she said. "You should marry him." She blinked and then reached for my face. "Look how pretty you are . . . my angel. You're my sweet angel." She went suddenly serious. "If it weren't for you, I'd be dead, you know."

My mother's fingers kept reaching, and so I leaned forward, took hold of them and pressed them to my cheek. Her eyes welled up until tears dribbled down.

You'd think, after everything, that Marlene would have given up hustling and drinking. That she'd have gotten religion— maybe joined a choir! Instead, it was me nosing around the church pews hunting for peace and someplace quiet.

It was going on three in the morning by the time we got back. Marlene giggled as Drew and I steadied her down the hall of our building. Coming through the apartment door she started to groan about being tired.

"I got to catch a few Zs," she said. "A few Zs!" she repeated, and laughed her head off.

I flicked the light on in our hall. Drew had never been in our apartment and now the dirt on the walls stood out in relief, the stains on the carpet, the stale smell of the place. He seemed to avert his eyes, trying not to look around.

Marlene suddenly grabbed Drew's chin and kissed his cheek with a loud smack. "Jesus Christ, you're cute," she said.

"You too," he told her. "I think we should put you to bed."

"Are you coming?" she asked.

"No," he said with a jittery laugh. "I have to go home."

"You can take off now," I said. "We're good." Drew stared at me and I looked away. "I mean it's late. You don't have to stick around."

Drew let Marlene's arm go as I pulled her toward her bedroom.

"Why is everybody leaving?" she said.

I didn't answer.

Her room smelled of stale booze. I didn't bother to turn the lights on as I shouldered her to the bed. I pulled the rumpled covers back and what sounded like a glass hit the rug, along with a few other bits of junk. I gave her a light shove and she squealed as she hit the mattress.

"*Show me the way to go home*," she sang, "*I'm tired and I want to go to bed.*" She interrupted herself with, "I'm hungry."

"Tough." I took off her shoes, hauled her legs onto the bed and yanked the covers over her.

After closing her door behind me, I went back into the hall to where Drew stood waiting.

"Do you want me to—?"

"Okay, well, thanks," I said, cutting him off as I headed for the front door.

"Are you going to be all right?" He glanced back at my mother's room and followed me.

"Yup. I'll talk to you later." Opening the door, I kept my eyes on the rug.

He paused, stuttering a little before he said, "Do you have, like, a social worker type thing? Because of the welfare?"

"No," I snapped. I forgot I'd told him about us being on welfare. But how else could I explain how we paid the rent? "I mean, some chick comes nosing around once a year to make sure we're not rich. But I'm not calling her."

"Maybe you should," he said. "I'm scared if you don't—" His eyes flicked away. "I'll talk to my mom. She—" Drew stuttered till his words went straight again. "Maybe you could sleep in my brother's old bed."

"That's very um—No, I'm—" I could feel my face getting hot. Drew came from people who were clean and good and right. I held the door open farther and kept my eyes away from his. "I'm okay. I'll talk to you later."

He stepped into the hallway, turned and looked at me. I should have said something more, but I just closed the door. Flicking off the light I leaned against the wall until I heard him moving down the hallway.

I haven't talked to Drew since. I can't look at him and I don't want him looking at me. I wish to hell I'd just left her in the drunk tank that night.

NINE

I WALKED AND walked, staring at the sidewalk, thinking of Drew. Plus what a fuck-up Marlene is these days. And when I look around me, I realize that after twenty minutes of walking, all I've done is get closer to her. I try to picture Ruby and Lou standing in my mother's living room. *Mind your own business, you tubby little dyke.*

When I get to Willingdon Avenue, I look across the street to the Old Orchard strip mall. The sun is breaking through the clouds and I'm beginning to sweat. I could really go for a drink. Maybe an Orange Crush. Ice cold. But the most immediate problem is money. That's frequently the most immediate problem. I'm only about five blocks from Marlene now.

It's not smart working close to home but sometimes you have to.

In the strip mall, outside the drugstore, I hang around the

garbage can till I can discreetly fish out a few cash-register receipts. My dad told me about this one—he used to do this when he was young and broke. You have to act normal, you can't make a big deal out of hunting for receipts or some uptight tool might notice and go squealing to a cop or something. The best one I find lists a pregnancy test, mascara, foundation, lipstick and blush. Total: $43.50. *Nice.* For appearance's sake, I snag an empty store bag too.

Inside the store, I lift the items off the shelves. Marlene would freak; she thinks shoplifting is totally low-class.

The problem with this scam, though, is you have to be exact. Not like when Sam was young. Ever since some stores started using barcode scanners instead of perfectly decent price tags, everything's gotten more complicated.

I have almost everything—the same pregnancy test, mascara, foundation and lipstick—but I can't find the right blush. *Shit!* I see the tag on the shelf but there's none left.

My heart starts to pound.

"Can I help you find something?"

Shit-shit! It's one of those cosmetic-counter ladies, wearing a dump truck's worth of makeup and frosty pink nails.

"No. I mean, yeah. I'm trying to find this, um, stuff and they're all, umm—" Smooth. What a loser.

"Oh, that shipment came in yesterday. I guess they haven't put them out yet," she says. "Can you wait just a moment?"

So I stand there and wait for her to bring me some blusher to steal. *God!*

When she gets back I choose the "English Suede" shade, thank her with this big phony smile, and take off to another aisle. When I take the store bag out of my pocket, my chest is banging so hard, I'm pretty sure I'm going to have a heart attack. I should put it all back. My legs are all wonky and wooden. I make myself go to the checkout.

I dump the pregnancy test and makeup on the counter and hand over the receipt. The cashier slaps down a pad of return slips. This is the *worst*—when you're freaking and you still have to close the deal. I take a deep breath, pull my hands out of my pockets, and write down a fake last name and number. As she reverses the charges and I take the cash, I start thinking about how disgusted my dad would be by this lame performance of mine.

"Sammie!"

My head snaps around. Jesus Christ. It's Drew, three people behind me in line.

I freeze a second. "Hey, how's it going?" I make a show of checking my watch as I head for the door. "I've got to go to the supermarket. For my mom."

"Wait!" His woolly blond lion hair hides his face as he counts out change to pay for a pack of gum. He told me once that he leaves his hair kind of long to distract from his big nose and his zits, but his skin's not that bad. And I like his nose.

I feel queasy and melty inside all at once.

"I'll be outside." I want to get out of here before a security guy's hand lands on my shoulder.

Out on the sidewalk, I try to remember this morning's dream. Something about fire. And Drew held my hand.

He comes out a few seconds later, and we head down the strip-mall sidewalk. The air between us is clunky.

"Where've you been?"

He's acting like it's no big deal, but I know he's mad. Before that shitty night when he drove me downtown, we talked on the phone nearly every day.

"I keep calling. But every time, your mom says you're not home."

"I've been really busy."

He nods. "You coming to the DYF roller party this Friday?" His voice is tight and the pitch is all wrong.

"Doubt it."

"When I called the last time," Drew tells me, "your mom said you were sleeping over at Jill's. I thought you didn't—I didn't think she was your type."

"We're not dating, for chrissake," I say, and roll my eyes as if he's the biggest moron. "What are you doing around here anyway?"

"Mandy organized this thing at her place this morning, making cookies for the Burnaby Seniors Centre."

"Mandy, Mandy. Quelle saint!"

Drew stops and stares at me. "Are you in trouble?"

I stop too. My chest clenches like a fist.

"A *pregnancy* test?" he whispers.

He saw. I look away and laugh.

Drew jams his hands in his pockets. He's got a loose long-sleeved T-shirt on but I can still make out the bones in his chest.

"I was taking it *back,* doofus."

"Your face is red," he says.

His is too.

My mind bugs around for an explanation. I hate lying to Drew, but he asks too many damn questions.

"You're such a goof." I laugh some more. "My mom bought it by mistake. She thought it was a douche. Okay? She's a total zone-out." I start down the strip again.

Drew catches up with me. "Why haven't you been returning my calls? Are you mad at me for something?"

"Nobody returns calls," I blurt. "I called my dad a couple weeks ago. He never called *me* back."

I wish I'd never said that. Now I can't shut up. "And he's my dad. But nope. That's life."

Drew trots to keep up. "Did you try calling him again?"

"Fuck him." I shove my way through the supermarket door.

"What?"

I turn and squint at Drew's face. "Fuck. Him."

I need some food to bring back to Ruby. People are less likely to throw you out if you bring home groceries once in a while. At the meat section, I grab a package of bacon. Don't even look at the price. Who cares? I watch my feet on the linoleum as I walk to the bread aisle.

Sappy Muzak dribbles through the store. Drew scrambles along beside me.

"That's crappy, Sammie. I'm—I'm sorry. I thought you were pissed with *me*. Did you talk to your mom about it?"

I snatch a loaf of grainy bread off the shelf, the kind with sesame seeds all over the crust—the kind they wrap in two plastic bags, it's so friggin' fancy—and start back toward the syrup aisle. Real maple syrup, Ruby, the good stuff. Suck on *that* tomorrow morning!

"Why the hell would I talk to *her* about it?"

I can't find the syrup. Just peanut butter and jam and my head is ready to explode.

I don't know what to do when I get like this. I don't know where to put it. This is why I don't want to talk to anyone right now. Least of all Drew.

"She was funny when I talked to her the other night," he says. "She thought someone had broken into the apartment and she kept saying, 'Who's there?' in this man-voice. She put the phone down a minute and went to check and then she came back on the line and said she had a hammer for protection." He laughs. "She wanted me to come over. She's like—"

I stop in the aisle and stare at him. "She wanted you to come *there*? To the apartment?" This is too much. He has to be bull-shitting. Maybe this is Drew getting even with me for ditching him all this time.

"She'd had a few. She didn't mean anything."

"Shut up."

"She kept saying, 'I need a man!'"

My hand shoots out and shoves him against the preserves. His face is shocked as he hits the shelf. A jam jar falls past his ear and busts open on the floor. It looks so horrible, the bloody red of it, like the inside of a skull. We both stare. A big goose egg sits in my throat and I can't swallow.

Drew looks at me. His mouth opens.

I take off for the cashiers. He doesn't follow. Who could blame him?

TEN

I GUESS THIS is Jill's idea of a good time—what the cool kids do, the ones who aren't "total suckholes." So far it seems like a drag.

It's midnight and I'm sitting on a log somewhere in the uncharted brush of deepest darkest Burnaby. Sparks from the bonfire pop now and then. The Byrne Road bush parties are a semi-regular event for Jill and her pals. The straight kids refer to them as Byrne Road Burnouts. This is the first time I've come out to one of these things.

Probably about twenty people down here. Maybe more. Kids wander in and out of the trees. Gabbing, necking, singing. On a log directly across the fire from me some dude who looks a little old for the crowd is playing guitar and singing "Let It Be" in a strained voice that would make any self-respecting dog howl his guts out. Three girls I recognize from school are gulping orange coolers from the bottle and singing along. Outside the ring of logs, a few guys pass a joint.

One of the orange cooler chicks falls off her log and the rest of them squeal and crack up and drag her back up off the ground.

Jesus. All these jerks want to do is get drunk and stoned. Like Marlene. What they don't get is, if you act like Marlene, you end up like Marlene. Fucked up and lonely and broke.

I've got a cherry Slurpee, nearly melted, that I've been nursing for the last couple hours. Nobody says a word to me. I'm just the little defective sitting on a log. The ultimate suckhole. Meanwhile, I know loan sharks, for chrissake! Fences! I've seen a gun! Not that I'm all superior about it, but *they're* the suckholes, not me. These people are clueless.

Jill and Crystal Norris are sitting on the dirt beside me, leaning back on the log, smoking and talking. Each of them holds a 7-Eleven Big Gulp cup. Lemonade and gin.

"Technically he broke up with me," Jill is saying. "But I was about to do it anyway."

"Why would you break up with Roman, man? He's a fox."

"Because all he wanted was one thing and *I* don't put out."

"*You're* a virgin?" Crystal says.

"Yes." Jill looks proud about it.

"You are such a lying hosebag!" Crystal laughs.

"I'm a *virgin*," Jill says emphatically.

"Where? In your left ear?" Crystal laughs even harder.

Crystal drove us here tonight. Her face had pinched up like a big anus the second we—I mean *I*—got into her car.

"Nobody told me it was Suckhole Night." She laughed, then said, "Just kidding."

We turned off Marine Drive and headed down another industrial road. I sat in the back and stared out the window, wondering why I'd agreed to come: nothing but gangly trees and scrubby weeds down here. No houses or apartments nearby. No phone booths. I don't think there's even a close bus stop. It's the kind of place where horror stories happen.

We parked on the side of the road behind a few other cars.

Crystal got out and tugged at the tight jeans climbing up her crotch. "These fuckin' Gloria Vanderbilts always give me camel-toe," she said.

"No kidding." Jill grimaced, and tugged at her jeans too.

Crystal walked ahead of us across the grass. At the top of the dirt path she stopped and pulled a bottle from her purse. "Let's just spike it now. Away from the moochers."

"Why'd you get *gin?*" Jill moaned. "Gin makes me wanna boke."

"It's all we got, so get over it," Crystal said. "Hold this." She shoved her lemonade cup into my hand while she twisted the cap off the gin. She stuffed the cap in the pocket of her purse and I held the cup while she popped the plastic lid and poured. She turned to Jill's.

I debated what to do if she wanted to spike mine. I wished I'd stayed home.

"Nobody'll mess with you," Jill had said. "You're with me."

Crystal turned back to me. "You going to take your lid off or what?"

I looked down at my two full hands.

Jill put her hand over my cup. "Sammie's on the wagon."

Crystal gave us one of her snide-twat snickers. Same laugh she laughed after she shoulder-checked me in the hall.

Jill switched her weight to the other hip and straightened to her full height. Bangles jangled down her wrist as she shoved one hand into her back pocket. "Listen, baby: She. Can't. Drink. You dig?"

Oh god. Full-on Foxy mode.

Screwing the cap back on the gin, Crystal sputtered with laughter. "Fuck off."

"What?" Jill stood a full head taller than Crystal. Her tight leather jacket opened to a scoop-neck T-shirt.

Crystal glanced at Jill's chest. Those big boobs of Jill's must seem like muscles to some girls.

"A.A.," Jill said, "do I have to spell it? Tuesday- and Thursday-night meetings. And now she's got A.M.A. meetings every Friday morning through the whole fucking summer."

"What the hell's A.M.A.?"

"Anger Management Anonymous?" Jill enunciated as if Crystal was a massive retard.

Crystal stared at me. "Seriously?" She stuffed the gin bottle back in her purse and said, "That's fucked up." She took her drink from my hand as she shot me another look. "You're seriously in anger management?"

"Fuckin' A," Jill said. "It's part of her probation. She broke some chick's *clavicle* last year." She took hold of Crystal's arm. "And by the way, Twelve Step groups are *seriously* anonymous.

So don't go shooting off your mouth. If I hear it from someone else, I'll know who it came from."

"Totally." Crystal tugged her arm back. "I'm not saying anything." She sucked on her straw, looking at me. Then she stopped drinking and said, "Well, I'll be dipped in shit!" Her mouth opened into a grin.

Jill gave me a quick wink and I looked away, embarrassingly teary with gratitude.

Now the two of them are sitting on the dirt, chain-smoking and talking their faces off, and I'm staring into the bonfire, my butt going numb on this log.

I can't stop thinking about the supermarket—that jam jar, the red, brainy meat of it lying beside Drew's foot. If my mother had jumped off the roof the night she promised to, I guess her skull would have busted open just like that.

Maybe I *should* be in anger management.

I look at Jill, her purple lips dark in the firelight. Cigarette smoke curls around her face. She's a better hustler than I would have thought. Better one than I am, probably.

Every now and then Crystal glances up. She's cross-legged and drunk and ever since Jill's performance at the top of the path, it's as if Crystal hopes I'll laugh at her jokes, agree with some remark she's made.

" . . . just like with Sammie," she's saying to Jill now. "I didn't used to get Sammie at all but it's like, you know, man, you see things in people that maybe other people don't, right."

Crystal looks so small down there in the dirt now—a blow-up monster that's been popped with a pin.

I'm so deep in thought, I don't notice anything's different until a German shepherd pokes his damp black nose in my face.

"Hi," I say, and touch his fur. He's excited, shoulders wiggling, sniffing the ground.

I look down, see shoes and realize that a cop's got hold of him on a leash. My stomach flips at the squeak of the cop's leather gun-belt. Have to remind myself that I don't have anything to worry about. I'm not drinking. There's nothing hot in my purse. No loaded dice, no marked cards. I am not Sam. I'm not Marlene.

The guitar playing stops.

I watch the dog trot from log to log, see the orange glow from the fire lighting up his coat and wish I could grab handfuls, push my face into his thick fur.

"Any open alcohol around here?" the cop calls out.

There's a second cop on the other side of the fire. He kicks a little sand into the flame.

A kid in a ball cap shoves something under a log with his foot and then sidesteps into a nearby group of guys.

The dog keeps sniffing here and there until he comes to that log, stops, barks and digs and barks some more. The dog-cop leans down and pulls a plastic sandwich bag out from under the log.

"Who does this belong to?" He shakes the baggy in the air. It looks empty but there's probably a bit of weed. He throws it into what's left of the fire.

"For fuck sakes," the kid in the ball cap hisses.

The second cop now has Crystal Norris's Big Gulp in his hand.

"Hey, man," Crystal says. "You got a warrant?"

He opens the cup, puts his nose in. "Whew!" he says. "Bad girl." He dumps the bit that's left into the sand.

"Fuckin' pigs," she mutters.

"Excuse me?" he says.

Jill has shoved her cup between her back and the log. She holds up empty hands.

"How about you?" the cop asks me.

I take the lid off my cup. "Cherry Slurpee. Straight."

He sniffs. "Good for you. The designated driver." He tips the dregs out anyway, looks around and yells, "Up and at 'em. Move it out and take your garbage with you."

The dog is still prancing, sniffing pant legs and purses.

Everyone is up off the ground now. Jill tries to tuck her cup into her jacket as she stands. The lid pops off and what's left dumps down the front of her jeans.

"*Motherfucker!*" She's covered in sticky lemonade and gin.

The cop with the dog laughs. "That's karma, kiddo."

We all plod back up the path toward the road.

"Holy shit, I'm wasted." Crystal giggles and grabs hold of my arm.

Jill takes Crystal's other arm. "Jesus, didn't you eat before you came out?"

Jill's a little drunk too, but nobody looks as bad as Crystal.

"Sure I ate. One piece of dry toast and half a grapefruit," Crystal slurs. "I'm doing this grapefruits diet, man. You should try it."

"Why," Jill asks her. "So I can be an assless wonder too?"

Crystal giggles. "You're just jealous. Do you know what size jeans I wear? Grapefruits, grapefruits, grapefruits."

The cop with the dog trudges behind us and the other one stands at the top of the path, giving us each the once-over.

As we pass him, Crystal holds up my hand and slaps her car keys into it. "Designated driver!"

When we find the car, Crystal gets into the passenger side. Jill sits in the back and takes out her cigarettes.

On the driver's side, I buckle my seat belt and stare ahead through the windshield for a couple seconds. "I don't have my licence," I say.

"You do so," Jill bellows from the back. I can hear her lighter flick and a quick inhale before she blows smoke and says, "You started going to those classes, like, the day you turned sixteen."

"Oh yeah!" Crystal squeals. "I saw you staying after school for driver's ed. I thought you were such a *fag*." She cackles her ass off and then in a booming announcer's voice says, "Young Drivers of Ca-na-da!"

I took those classes all right. I caught the bus way out to the east burbs—Coquitlam, Port Coquitlam, Port Moody—so I could pull off enough drugstore returns for the fee. They held the in-class stuff in Mr. Walters' Trades Math room. Then we did another three weeks of actual driving in one of those freaky cars with two steering wheels. I loved it. Driving was like growing wings. I was determined to get my licence. Then things went off the rails with Marlene.

I turn the ignition.

Crystal screams. "Fuckin' Sammie! You don't care about

anything! You're so fuckin' cool." She looks over at me with watery eyes and slurs, "Seriously, Sammie. I just didn't get you before, but you're . . ."

Jill pushes her head between the front seats. "She's the baddest chick in town."

Peels of laughter from Crystal. "Foxy fuckin' Brown!"

I'd like to slap Crystal. I can almost feel the heat of the slap in my palm as I adjust the rear-view mirror.

I'd give anything to have Drew with me now. Drew has his licence. An image of him flashes in my mind, bent over the steering wheel, carefully putting his father's car into drive.

ELEVEN

I'M ON THE couch with Jill. It's one-thirty in the afternoon and we're still not dressed because it's pouring today. Pissing sideways.

I'm kind of happy, though.

Lou came home from work a minute ago. He stood here in the living room, taking up the entire door frame, and said, "Sammie, I understand you had to drive the girls home from a party the other night. Some drinking involved." He scowled at Jill.

"*Daddy!* It was Crystal, not me!" Jill sounds like a six-year-old in a tutu when she sugar-talks her dad.

Lou looked back at me. "I just want to say that I appreciate you trying to do the responsible thing, Sammie. But I don't want you driving without a licence. So if you want to make an appointment to take your road test this week, I'd be happy to give you a lift." Then he lowered his head in that funny, bashful way he has and went upstairs.

I feel as if I've got sparklers in my gut right now. Nobody else except maybe those born-again kids talks like Lou, makes out like I'm a good girl, a dignified kind of person.

"Sammie, you're blushing." Ruby smirks. She's sitting kitty-corner to us on the other couch, sewing the hem on a pair of Lou's pants.

Whenever a person tells me I'm blushing, it just gives me an even bigger lobster-face. Lou's so nice it's embarrassing.

Jill is in her fuzzy purple bathrobe. I'm in my pyjamas and a beat-up University of British Columbia sweatshirt that once belonged to Jill's ex-boyfriend, Roman. Roman used to play basketball for UBC but he was flunking so they kicked him out. He was way older than Jill. Twenty-two. I asked Jill once why Ruby let her go with a guy that old and she said, "I do what I want no matter what she says. And she'd rather know the truth than have me lie."

Staring at the TV screen, Jill says, "Man, is Billy Dee Williams not the finest looking man you ever saw?"

We're watching some old movie called *Mahogany*.

He looks a bit slick if you ask me. Like a hustler who doesn't know enough to downplay it. "What else has he been in?"

"You never saw *Lady Sings the Blues?*" Jill says, as if I must've been raised by wolves.

She's got the soundtrack from *Lady Sings the Blues* in her bedroom. The *Mahogany* one too. Diana Ross singing her guts out. Jill must have a dozen Diana Ross albums.

"If I married him," Jill says, mooning at the TV, "I wouldn't even have to change my last name. *Jill Williams, meet Billy Dee*

Williams. *Why, hello, Jill. You are one hot mama and I think
we would have beautiful babies together.*"

"Better watch it," I tell her. "Maybe he's not just any brother.
Maybe he's *your* brother."

Ruby titters. "I think I'd remember that," she says.

Hardly any black people live in Burnaby. Or Vancouver either.
There are only two black kids in our whole school, which is
probably why Jill's so fascinated—she thinks it's exotic.

I wonder what Jill's dad thinks. My dad is pretty weird about
black people. His friends are too. Marlene told me about this
thing that happened before I was born. She said that she and
Sam were over for drinks at another couple's place: Peggy and
Mike. Peggy—she's now with my dad—was going out with a
loan shark called Mike McGee back then. They were sitting
around drinking wine and talking about how the white neigh-
bour lady had gotten married to a black man.

Peggy didn't think it was such a big deal.

Her boyfriend, Mike, said, "That sounds okay to you?
Would you sleep with one of 'em?"

Peggy said that it depended.

"Would you sleep with a nigger or not? Answer the
question."

Marlene flashed her a look, trying to signal Peggy to say no.

But Peggy answered, "Maybe if I fell in love with one of 'em."

Mike slapped Peggy in the mouth. Then he grabbed her by the
hair, dragged her off her chair and called her a whore and a slut.

Marlene and Sam got out of there. Peggy was on the floor
and Mike was waving a gun around before they left the house.

I wish I hadn't thought of that. Makes me think I *was* raised by wolves.

Sitting here in the living room now, I watch Ruby's sewing needle poke in and out of Lou's jeans. Lou would never talk the way Sam and his friends do.

Diana Ross is singing on TV, asking whether you know where you're going to and if you know what life is showing you. I hate this song. It's the most depressing song ever written. It doesn't even have a proper title, just "Theme from *Mahogany*."

Jill is warbling along.

This song is an even bigger drag than "Knocking on Heaven's Door," and *that* is an all-time wrist-slasher if I ever heard one.

The doorbell rings.

Jill looks at her mother. Her mother looks back.

"You get it," they say in stereo. Then they both turn to me. "Sammie, you get it."

The two of them are still giggling their asses off when I get up and open the door.

Standing on the porch is Drew, soaking wet.

My stomach drops as if I'm flying down the first hill on a roller coaster.

"What are you *doing* here," I whisper, slip outside onto the welcome mat and pull the door behind me. Beyond the overhang, rain is pelting the steps.

"I looked up Jill in the phone book."

I can just make out that stupid shitty *Mahogany* song still plinking away in the living room. *When you look behind you,* Diana says, *there's no open door. What are you hoping for?*

"I was going to just phone you but—" Drew pauses. "That thing in the supermarket, I just—" He sputters, *"P-p-p,"* as if he can't make words for a second or two. "What's wrong with you? Why did you do that?"

"I'm sorry. I'm—" I feel the goose egg in my throat again. It's ready to burst. Inside the house: *Do you know where you're going to?* Over and over. I can't talk.

"I don't get you. What did I do?"

"It's not about *you.* I've got other stuff going on." I look down at the weather-beaten porch between my bare feet. "I'm not even dressed."

He looks away, shaking his head like he can't believe it. For a second I think he's going to walk down the stairs, back into the rain, and be done with me.

Instead he says, "I came here because you're not home. I mean—" He sighs as if he's collecting himself. "I thought I should find you because, um, because I think something's wrong with your mom. She called my place yesterday at, like, five in the morning. My mother answered and told her I was still sleeping. So then she called again at seven. My mom was so mad." He laughs nervously because Drew and his mom don't get along.

Then there's a long pause until he says, "She was pretty revved up. She had this whole idea—your mom—about making you famous. I'm supposed to take a picture of you with tons of pink roses in a pink Cadillac. She said she drew me an illustration. Everything has to be pink for it to work. Then we're supposed to send the picture to Phil Donahue, the talk-show guy. Everyone in the plan is Scottish, she said, so it would work because of the pattern. Because you're Scottish, and I'm Scottish, and she's Scottish and Phil Donahue's Scottish . . ."

I move past him to edge of the porch. A drop of cool rain slants in and snaps my face. I wrap my arms around my ribs. I shouldn't even have a friend like Drew. Drew is going to heaven. Me and Marlene are not.

He leans against the railing. "She kept asking if I could see the pattern. It was like she'd decoded the pattern and she could see it and nobody else could. Um. I said that sounded neat or interesting or whatever. Maybe we could talk about it later. So, I called her last night to see how she was doing and she had a whole other plan about making a million dollars. It had to do with pills and doctors and this secret code on pill bottles. She said it would work because of everybody being Chinese. She's Chinese and so is her doctor."

I turn around. "She who? My mother is Chinese?"

"Yeah. And some guy named Freddy."

I look out at the rain hitting the parked cars and the side-walk and the road.

"Sammie?"

"Yup."

"Are you okay?"

"Yup."

"Do you want to hang out? Go for coffee? Or we could take the bus downtown . . . go to Stanley Park maybe. Lost Lagoon is kind of cool when it's raining."

Across the road, there is a car parked with a small cargo trailer hitched to the back. I wish I could climb inside the trailer part. I want to be where it's small and dark and closed. Where no one can see me or hear me.

"Sammie?"

"I can't."

"Okay. Well, uh, well, I have something for you. It's just this, um, poem." He pulls a folded envelope out of his jacket pocket. He goes to hand it to me. The edges are wet. "Or I could just read it to you now. Should I?" He goes quiet again. "Sammie?"

I feel my chest caving when he says my name.

I wish I were mean and strong. I wish I could punch Marlene for this and Drew too, bust everything apart. But I just stand here on the porch, sucking inside-out instead.

"I love you," Drew says.

Like getting my head held under water. Like a pillow pressed over my face.

I shake my head no, walk back into the house, and close the door behind me, leaving him there on the stoop holding his folded poem.

TWELVE

RAIN IS COMING down so hard it's bouncing off the sidewalks. No umbrella. Cold drops snap my skin and stream down my face, inside the collar of my jacket, down my spine. I don't care. Let it wash me away.

Before I left the house, Jill came downstairs to find me hiding in her bedroom. I had wiped my face but she could see my red eyes. "Who was that outside?"

"Drew. Is he gone?"

"Yeah. He went trudging down the steps like someone just drop-kicked him." She sat beside me on her bed, almost whispering. "Did you guys break up?"

"He's not my boyfriend."

"Did he say something shitty to you?"

"I want to go home."

"Oh, Sammie." She put a purple fuzzy bathrobe arm around

my shoulders and tried to hug me close. "It's going to be okay. Come on, Sam."

"Don't call me that." I pulled away. "I'm not Sam."

Ruby clomped down the stairs and pushed the beaded curtain aside. "What's wrong? Who was that outside?"

"Her friend, Drew. She wants to go home."

"Sammie honey, that's not a good idea." Ruby came into the room.

"I want it how it *was*," I said. I got up off the bed and folded my arms. "There's *nothing* now. It's all *nothing*."

Ruby put her arms around me and squeezed. I went stiff and tried to wriggle away from her round soft self. She hugged tighter.

When she finally eased her grip, she said, "You don't like to be touched, do you, Sammie. Seems as if you didn't grow up with much affection. Don't you need a hug now and then?"

Why does everyone think they know what the hell I need?

I had loads of affection. Maybe not from Sam, but Marlene was a blue-ribbon mush-pot, always petting and kissing me. When I was a kid sometimes I slept in the same bed with her. Especially when we were on the road, Marlene, Sam and me—Sam didn't want to spring for an extra bed. Late at night, Marlene used to play a game where she wrote words on my back with her finger and I had to guess what she'd just written. It felt so yummy to have my back tickled that I would slide into a stupor every time.

"I don't know," I'd say, "write it again. Write me a book."

Made me want to bawl thinking of it there in Jill's bedroom, Marlene's fingernails grazing my skin.

"I'm going out," I told Ruby.

Jill glanced at her mother. "Do you want company?"

"I'm not going home, okay, I just want to go for a walk."

Ruby's tone went low and careful. "I don't know what all's happened to you, Sammie, but I just want you to know that we love you."

Jesus Christ! Love, love love.

Anyone who says *I love you* is just trying to hold you hostage. Drew should knock it the hell off, too, I thought. He should take it back.

And just like that, the phone rang again. Ruby, Jill and I looked at the bedside table. Ruby picked up, said hello and listened.

"Just a moment." She held the receiver out for me.

"Sammie?" Drew's voice was strained and huffing, as if he'd been running. He must have been at a phone booth. I could hear the traffic. "I'm sorry. I meant like a friend. You're my best friend. Like that, okay? I love you like that."

"I have to go," I said, and hung up the phone.

————

Rainwater drips off the ends of my hair. People passing by with umbrellas look at me as if I'm a complete berserker, out in a downpour like this.

Is it turkeys that tilt their heads back in the rain and drown?

I keep hearing Drew. *I love you.* Marlene too. *I love you.* Makes me want to dig out my skull with a spoon.

Marlene claims to be selective about the love stuff. She doesn't say that to just anyone, she says. Mind you, she also says, "Tell the truth and shame the devil," whenever she's trying to get something out of me. She hates all that God stuff and then she comes out with crazy shit like that.

I love you, Marlene says, and then she buggers off and doesn't even leave a note. It was just her and me. Me and her. She used to *understand* that. She used to *always* leave notes.

One time, I heard her out back at two in the morning with some jerk. My mother has the worst taste in men.

"Come on, Jack, just for a minute," she kept saying. Her *s*'s were sliding all over the place. The guy's voice was too low to make out. Marlene got louder. "Look at me, Jack, please?" Right outside my bedroom window.

Made me sick to hear her beg like that. I pulled the pillow over my head.

Suddenly, clippy footsteps came down the little cement path beside our balcony. And then I heard the Romanian accent of Nadia, the caretaker's wife.

"Marlene!" she said in a loud whisper. "You are waking up half the building."

I wondered why it was Nadia and not her husband, George, coming out in the middle of the night. Seems like Nadia always had to do the dirty work.

"This is *my* goddamn place," my mother said to Nadia, "and I'll do whatever the hell I like."

I peered through the crack between the curtains. I saw parts of Nadia—short, choppy hair, pyjama pants, and her elbow jumping around in a woolly sweater as she jabbed a finger toward Marlene.

"Get inside your goddamn place," Nadia hissed, "or I will call the police!"

Then the jerk spoke up. "Let's calm down."

"Don't tell me what to do!" That was Marlene, of course.

I listened until our apartment door opened and closed. There was scuffling and bumping, my mother saying, *Oops*, and giggling.

I tried to let my brain fade into sleep. After a while, my mom's voice came high and needy again, like a baby, like a Siamese cat.

"I love you, Jack. I *love* you."

That was the capper.

"I never even said *I love you* to your father," Marlene had once told me. "Only you. The second you were born I loved you."

I'd never even heard of Jack.

I opened my bedroom door and stood there, looking into the living room, where my mother was on the couch pawing the guy's face. Jack was all leathery brown and skinny like a science project. I swear to God, he was like one of those bog-men who gets preserved in peat for a hundred years.

"Mom!"

She jerked around. "Sammie." Her voice went all honey-pie. "Come here." She patted the bit of empty couch beside her. "Jack, this is my little girl."

"Hello," the bog-man said. Long, bony fingers wiggled the air toward me.

"You want to keep it down? I've got school in the morning."

Marlene often says it's my tone that pisses her off, not the words. She'd slapped my face once last year for my tone. I'd looked at her with this hard, amused expression that I'd been working on, and she ran like hell into her bedroom and slammed the door. I could hear her dresser drawer rattle as she rooted around for something that would take the edge off.

Now, her mouth hung open for a good three seconds before she blurted, "You slept *last* night. You're *always* sleeping."

"Are you for real?" I said.

I went back to my room and closed the door. Leaning against it, I listened as Jack made noises about leaving. Marlene told him she loved him again. Jack left.

I refused to speak to her the next morning.

She didn't notice; she was sleeping.

After school that day, Nadia was outside our open door as I came down the hallway. Her voice was sharp and she was jabbing a finger at Marlene.

My mother kept her arms crossed.

Nadia's expression changed into a smile for me. I tried to make nice as I slipped past her to my mother's side of the door.

As soon as I was by her, Nadia went back to that harsh sneer. "You think you can wake up half the building and nothing is going to happen? Not so!"

"Where's George? When I signed the rental agreement for this godforsaken hole, I signed it with *George*." No matter her history, Marlene figures a guy will always treat you better. She'll go to the longest line in the supermarket just to deal with a guy.

"*George!* George has *had* it with you. He'd have kicked you out a long time ago except he likes Samantha. He thinks she's cute. Lucky for you."

Marlene's mouth hardened. "That *is* lucky," she said. If she'd been a cat, her tail would have been switching, hard.

My lungs clenched.

"If I have to speak to you again, no more chances!" Nadia gave me another gruesome smile before she hurried away, her tough little legs zipping down the hallway.

I made a beeline for my room.

Marlene followed me. "*George thinks Sammie's cute!* Isn't she cute with those trashy tight jeans painted on her teenaged ass? Cutest thing you ever saw." Then she stormed into the kitchen and slammed things around in the sink.

"What do you figure that little bitch meant by *that?* You and George spending time together these days or what?"

I came out and stood in the kitchen entrance. "No. I told you—he's a drama coach. He gave me his business card because he thinks I should be an actress. He thinks I'm interesting."

"I'll bet," she said. "I'll just fucking bet. Maybe cute Sammie could haul her interesting ass in here and clean up the kitchen!"

———

I'm standing in the phone booth now. I have to call one of them and I don't know which one first.

I stick in a quarter.

Seems to ring and ring forever.

Finally, "Hello?" Her tone sounds urgent, as if she's been interrupted in the middle of performing brain surgery.

"Mom? It's me."

She breathes out a bitchy kind of disgust. I can almost hear her lip curl.

"What's going on? Is everything okay?"

"You tell me," she says.

"Excuse me?"

"*Excuse me?*" she mimics.

"What are you *doing?* What's *wrong* with you?"

"You think you're going to run off with him and just leave me here in the muck? You and Freddy. What a laugh."

"Freddy?"

"The *index* card!" she says. "I *found* it, smartass. In the living room. Think you're so damn smart. There's code scratched all over it—I can *read* it."

I stand in the phone booth, rain dribbling down the outside of the glass as I try to put it all together. The thought of Freddy's face up-close makes me want to puke. Then the index card flutters through my brain onto the couch: me in the living room, calling all over town. I forgot to put the card back. It probably slipped down between the couch cushions.

"I called him because I was looking for *you.*"

"See how far you get!" She hangs up.

Leaning in the phone booth, I watch little rivers run down Kingsway. Brown puddle-waves splash the sidewalks as cars rush by.

THIRTEEN

"HAVE I REACHED Samantha Bell? Hello, Samantha, this is Jean White calling. I'm a counsellor from Oak Shore Mental Health. We're calling to let you know that your mother, Marlene, was admitted here three days ago. I understand you are no longer living at home but we thought we should be in touch."

"Mental health? Is that like . . . an insane asylum?"

"No, not quite like that." Her voice reminded me of a school secretary's: stick-up-the-butt polite. "Your mother's been having some troubles so she has a bed here until she's feeling better. If you'd like to see her, our visiting hours are 1p.m. to 4 p.m."

———

I'm sitting outside the main building now, on one of their benches, staring up at steely block letters over the doors: OAK

SHORE MENTAL HEALTH. It was easy to get to by bus. Right off Willingdon Avenue. Which is peculiar when you think about it. Willingdon is a pretty busy street. I thought when people had nervous breakdowns, they needed somewhere a little more quiet.

The place doesn't look that bad. It's not a giant cement psycho-centre, with bars on the windows, the way you see in movies. Looks more like an old elementary school, stucco and wood.

I told them I'd be here at one o'clock. It's twenty after.

Just when you think a situation is as fucked up as it can get, the fucked-up-itude still manages to knife you in the back.

I don't know if Marlene is going to be walking the halls in one of those white jackets with the wraparound sleeves or what. It's my fault if she is. If I'd just stayed put, maybe I could've snapped her out of it. But nope, I buggered off. And that's what happens when you leave a person alone—they go sour. Like milk.

Why didn't she call me herself?

What if they're doing awful things to her in there?

I think I'm going puke.

No puking. Grow up.

I stand up finally and head for the door.

Inside, it's like a cross between a hospital and a hotel. The linoleum is cream with brown wisps—shiny, as if it gets polished every day.

At the front desk, I tell them I'm here for Marlene. The receptionist is older with perfect makeup, hair very smooth and neat. When she smiles, she reveals rows of straight white teeth. She looks sort of high-class, which makes me feel better.

Marlene likes women who look high-class. She always hates it if I use bad grammar or rounder slang because of how low-class it sounds. Half the time that Marlene criticizes what I'm wearing, it's that type of issue. "Take that off, you look like a low-life." She doesn't seem to notice so much with men. Or maybe she just forgives them for it.

The receptionist tells me Marlene's room number and points me down the hall. I was expecting electronic doors or something. I thought I would have to be buzzed through Security.

The door of room 126 is open. I stop outside and pull my shirt smooth. Peering inside, I see Marlene sitting there on a single bed, looking into her compact, wiping lipstick from the corners of her mouth.

I tap my nails on the door. "Hello?"

"Oh." She fumbles her compact shut. "It's you." When she says *you,* her voice sounds warm and scared together.

She chucks the compact into her purse, rubs her palms over her slacks and gets up. She looks beside her and around the room and back at me as if she doesn't know what to do next. "Well," she says, and takes a step.

I take a step too and we look at each other and then one of us puts out her hands and the other one does the same and we stand there holding each other's fingers, both of us nervous, as if we're standing in a dark alley.

"Are you skipping off today?" She smiles a little.

She means "skipping out." The first time I told her I skipped out on a class, she thought it was hilarious. She pictured me skipping off down the street, she said.

"Summer vacation," I remind her.

"Right." She shakes her head and looks away. "Are you hungry? There's a cafeteria we could go to on the second floor."

I say no even though I could eat. I can't stop eating lately. My jeans are getting hard to zip.

"There's a common room too. With a TV. Or we could just sit here and, uh . . . sit here." A hand goes to her temple, tugs some hair and pulls it behind her ear.

"Here's fine," I say, and sit down in the chair against the wall.

Marlene sits on the skinny bed. Her skin looks as if I could poke a finger through it. There is a slight tremor in her hands. She sees me looking and folds them in her lap.

"So," she says. "Everything's okay where you're staying? I didn't have the number to uh, uh . . ."

"Jill's?"

"*Jill's*. The counsellor knew where to find you. I guess she called Social Services and they had it."

I pick at the arm of the chair. "Jill's mom got them to put her down as my temporary guardian. That way she gets child welfare money for looking after me."

"Oh." Marlene's mouth opens again and hangs that way for a couple seconds. "I guess everything's okay there?"

"Yup. I'm going to take the road test for my driver's licence this week. Lou's taking me."

"Lou?" She repeats the name as if it makes her sad and confused.

"Jill's dad. You met him."

"I did?"

"Ruby and Lou. They went over to the apartment to look in on you."

"Right." Something like fear flashes across her eyes again. "That woman."

"Ruby."

She shakes her head and takes a big breath. "I'm sorry, I—"

"I called you a few days ago. Do you remember that?"

She stares. Her look is buggy and shiny like a cat's when it's hiding under the bed.

"You thought I was going to run away with Fat Freddy," I remind her. "You said there was code scratched into the Freddy file card and that's how you knew."

Marlene closes her eyes.

Maybe I shouldn't have said it so bluntly.

She keeps her eyes shut when she says, "I found that index card in the living room. I guess I got mixed up." She glances out the window. "The last time I talked to Freddy he said you were turning into a nice-looking little broad."

"Ew. He hasn't seen me since I was, like, thirteen or something. Dumb-ass."

She turns her head to me. "Did you just say *dumbass?*"

I shrug, smile. Must've picked that one up from Jill.

Her eyelids flutter and she smirks. "He's a *dumbass* all right. Maybe he *didn't* say it. Maybe I dreamed it. It's hard to know what was . . . I remember people watching me from the TV. And the window blind . . . signalling." She gestures with two hands as though she's working the blind strings, opening and closing them. Taking a shaky breath, she looks into her hands, and picks at some chipped polish on her fingernail. "I didn't think you'd ever leave me."

"You said you were going to kill yourself. You said you didn't want me to have to find you."

"I don't *blame* you. I just didn't think you would. Seemed like I was really finished if *you* left. I dumped the last of the vodka and the rest of the tranquilizers. And then I had a grand mal seizure. Right in the middle of the Mac's Mini-Mart. Ambulance came . . . the hospital gave me Dilantin for the seizures and a prescription for more Valium. Or Ativan. I forget . . . I went back home and downed the whole bottle. Apparently George found me out cold in the lobby and called an ambulance."

"The lobby in our building?"

She nods, puts her palms on the edge of the bed and pushes herself up straight. She runs her teeth over her bottom lip and says, "What did I say to you? Something awful . . ."

"You told Drew about a plan to make me famous with a pink Cadillac and pink roses."

She looks embarrassed and suddenly I'm not sure if I'm picking on her about the Cadillac stuff or trying to say something nice. If you think about it, it was pretty decent of her to want to make me famous.

"You wanted to send a picture of me in a pink car with the roses to Phil Donahue because he was Scottish. It was only going to work if all the stuff was pink and all of us were Scottish."

Marlene's not Scottish. Sam is. I'm half.

"Isn't Donahue Irish?" she asks.

I snort and so does she. We're both looking for a place to make a joke but nothing quite works yet. Or maybe it's just not funny any more.

I suck in air until my chest hurts and then let it out. "How long do you have to stay here?"

Marlene keeps looking into her hands. "I thought they were going to send me home. I didn't want to go. I guess I panicked. We had a group session and I—" She covers her face with both palms for a second and then puts them down. "I put green eye shadow all over my face. To prove—So they'd see that I definitely . . ."

I look at her. "Seriously?"

She tucks in her lips like a kid who's been caught swiping pennies. "Group went on like nothing happened. Nobody said a word. Maybe I didn't put on as much as I thought. They didn't send me home, though."

"Jesus Christ."

Marlene opens her eyes wide, spreads her lips and gives me a crazy fake smile—like one of those old wind-up monkeys with the banging cymbals. Then suddenly we start to giggle, and even when we stop, the nerves in my guts flutter and I'm afraid that if I don't force some more laughter I'm going to bawl instead.

FOURTEEN

I DIDN'T STAY in Marlene's room that long. Couldn't stand the clumsy feeling, as if she and I don't really know each other any more. I liked the part where we laughed about group therapy. But we shouldn't have. Christ, she's painting her face green to prove she's nuts enough to stay in the nuthouse.

When I left Oak Shore, I didn't want to get back on the bus either. Didn't want strangers gawking at me. Feels like you can read it all over me: Loser Orphan Annie. So I'm walking home—no, I'm walking back to Jill's.

At least last week I could imagine that Marlene missed me and wanted me there with her. And Sam. Where the hell is Sam?

Drew keeps climbing into my head. I hear him say *I love you* again and my insides feel squirmy with it. Thing is, he was probably telling the truth the second time he called—he didn't mean it like *that,* he meant it as a friend. He loves me in that

Jesus-y way. Not like a guy. The only guys who ever think of me *that* way are old perverts like Fat Freddy.

I'm staring at the sidewalk, moving on autopilot. Midway through July and now that the rains have stopped, it's summer for real. The sun is so hot and heavy my clothes are sticking to my skin. These jeans are too tight; it's a workout just to walk in them.

When I look up, I realize that I'm on Sardis Street—almost at our building. Like a homing pigeon. I don't know why I'm going here. Part of me expects to walk into the apartment and see Marlene and me sitting in front of the boob tube just like old times.

We used to have a blast making fun of crap on TV. The best was watching glitzy beauty pageants—*Miss Universe, Miss America*. We'd heat up a frozen pizza and pop some kind of fizzy drinks and we'd time it so that everything would be ready before the show started. When the pageant music began, I'd always yell, "Release the hounds!" Marlene would laugh every time I said it.

Later on in the show, I might ease up and say something like, "Miss Texas is pretty."

"Pretty good at fetching papers," Marlene would answer. "Look at Illinois, I think she's smuggling pumpkins in her pants."

We'd laugh our heads off.

I guess I kind of *do* want to go home. I want to see for myself how messy it is. Plus, I need more clothes.

I always cut through the little path in the shrubs at the rear of the building to get to our apartment on the ground floor. But I feel like a burglar doing it now. What if I run into George or Nadia? I wonder if the rent is paid up. I wish I could just slip over the railing and go in through the sliding glass door, but it's locked from the inside.

When I get to our patio, I stand there for a second, hand on the railing, squinting into the living room. Can't see anything; the curtains are pulled tight.

Eventually, I walk down the cement path to the back door. I keep still in the corridor a few seconds, listening for footsteps or movement. The building is dead quiet.

Rushing down the hall, I jam my key in the lock.

When our door opens, the garbage-stink hits me like a truck. The place is sweltering. I check the thermostat. Holy shit, Marlene had it cranked up to eighty. I pull it back twenty degrees.

In the kitchen, dishes are piled up and the tap is dripping, one splat at a time on the top plate. It's not *that* terrible. Definitely reeks, though. I open the cupboard under the sink. Fruit flies rise in a cloud and waft out into the air around me. The garbage pail is full and rotting.

Ruby tsks in my head, *Disgusting.* I'd like to see Ruby pause to take out the garbage before they load *her* onto a stretcher.

Batting fruit flies out of my face, I pull the pail out onto the floor, grab the ends of the bag and pick it up like a dirty diaper. The Dumpster is in the basement. I hate going down there. Creeps me out.

———

The cool cement of the garage sends a jolt up my bare feet into my shinbones. The slap of each step echoes around the walls. I glance over my shoulder, thinking about all the horrible rape stories that take place in underground parking lots—and slam face-first into George.

"Hello, Sammie," he says.

Up close like this, George is enormous, a wall.

"And what are you doing with bare feet, you little rascal?" He reaches out and slaps my butt.

A stupid laugh comes out of me. I skitter away toward the Dumpster.

"Sammie-girl, how is your mother? She's still in the hospital, yes?"

"She's better." The bag drips as I chuck it into the big steel bin. "She just had a—She fainted." I head back to the door.

"Are you home all alone?" George's voice echoes.

"She's fine."

He walks alongside me. "You give any more thought about the class?" His eyebrows form an A-frame over his glasses. "I told you that I'm coaching the drama, yes?"

He's told me—about a hundred times. He complained that he used to coach great theatre actresses in Romania, but here all anyone wants to do is get acting jobs on crappy TV shows. If he's so great, how come he's stuck managing *this* dump?

"Thinking about it."

"Don't waste time thinking," he says as he plucks my wrist up. "You got something." My hand is sandwiched between both of his now. "I know what I'm talking about. You have great potential."

I catch his wink through the tinted glasses he always wears.

"Ha ha," I say, and pull my hand back. Marlene would be pissed off with me for not telling him to eff off. But I'm not sure if he's technically done anything that bad. Plus, there's the fact that George is the only thing standing between us and the street.

I reach the basement door and unlock it. "I'll ask my mom."

Pulling the door open for us, he follows me into the hall. "We'll work it out, Sammie-girl," he says, and pats my shoulder with a heavy thump.

I step away as he pokes the elevator call button. "I'm gonna take the stairs," I say. "I'll see you."

I slip into the stairwell and run two at a time back up to the ground floor.

———

In the living room I open the sliding door and the windows and then go back into the kitchen and open up the fridge: nothing much here. The cheese that Ruby and Lou bought. Milk's about to expire. In the freezer there's a loaf of bread. I throw a slice in the toaster.

These jeans are cutting off my circulation. Probably why I can't think straight: I'm strangling from the waist down. I undo the zipper and head for my bedroom.

Once my shorts are on and my sweaty socks off, I grab a duffle bag and start chucking in underwear and T-shirts. The floppy straw hat that Drew gave me for my birthday last year is scrunched on the floor of the closet. I'm lonesome just looking at it. I put it on my head. The smell of the straw reminds me of Drew at the Hollow Tree Ranch. *You're bad. You ain't seen nothin' yet.*

The toast pops. Back in the kitchen, there's no clean knife. I wash and dry one quick, grab the peanut butter and slather it on, take a big bite and feel better.

Back at the open balcony door, I take in fresh air and look at the shrubs and trees, and try to feel normal. Now that I'm here, I don't want to be. I want to be back at Jill's where it's clean. Not cleanliness clean. I mean where it doesn't feel dirty with bad memories.

Once I've popped the last of the toast in my mouth I head back to the kitchen. *"Dirty dishes piled in the sink and on the counters. How can she live like that?"*

There's still a jungle's worth of fruit flies staggering through the air. I walk over to the counter, pick up the soap and squirt some over the pile of dishes. The washcloth is hard and crusty.

I turn on the hot water. It ricochets off the top plate and gets me in the face. *Shit!* I swing the tap to the side. There's barely room to rinse one cup. But I start in anyway. We're not pigs, Ruby. We just have a lot to contend with.

That's what Marlene always says. *We have a lot to contend with.* I used to like it when she said that. Made me feel as if we were put-upon in a sophisticated sort of way. She said it to Mr. Walters when he called to complain that I'd skipped out.

That happened when Sam was in town last, when I was feeling shitty about how it had all played out.

———

Sam had already been in town a few days when he called. I think he often waits until the last minute to decide if he feels like seeing me.

I had started grade 11 a couple of months before, so he offered to take me shopping. Kind of a combined birthday present/new school clothes thing. Didn't have to ask me twice. Better than the alternative: just before I started grade 9, he mailed me a bunch of clothing but it was all girls' size 10/11—as if he thought I was still a little kid.

My dad never sends any kind of child support whatsoever. I guess he feels he has to witness each purchase. He told Marlene once that there was no point in sending her cash—she would just drink it all away. That used to piss me off; now I think he might have had a point.

I asked him if we could go to Pacific Centre Mall in Vancouver. He didn't see the reason. Why deal with the hassle of parking downtown, he said, when all the Burnaby stores have the same stuff.

Easy for him to say. He gets to be downtown whenever he feels like it.

So we drove ten minutes to Brentwood Mall. Sam stood around in his crisp orange shirt and his fancy creased slacks while I yanked on pair after pair of jeans. I kept looking at that orange shirt of his. In the expensive stores, they don't say "orange," they say "apricot." Marlene said he gets a lot of his stuff tailor-made.

He watched me stand in the mirror, inspecting each pair of jeans. He frowned a lot. "Aren't those too tight? How can you sit down in pants that tight?"

Sam is pretty out of it in that department. Jill has to lie down on her bed to do up her fly every morning. Jill said Crystal Norris has to lie down, take a wire hanger and hook it through the zipper tab so she can get the fly up without ripping the crap out of her fingers.

Sam bitched, but he still took me from store to store and bought me whatever I asked for: a new bomber jacket with a sheepskin collar, jeans, tops, running shoes, sweatshirts and a sharp-looking charcoal grey pantsuit because I said I might apply for a Christmas job.

Early on in the spree, he asked about whether I needed "panties."

Jesus Christ, he said *panties!* I hate when guys say that word. They sound like skeevy old perverts.

Pass! No thanks. I wasn't about to get new undies with him around anyway. Let's face it: I barely knew Sam any more.

He also toured me around the drugstore and bought me tons of stuff that Marlene hates to spend money on like wheat-germ-oil-and-honey shampoo, baby-powder-scented deodorant, Noxzema and zit cream.

We were probably together two or three hours but we barely spoke. He asked a few monosyllabic questions: *How's school?*

How's your grades? Got a plan for later? By "later," he meant after I graduated high school.

Nope. Not exactly.

Mr. Walters and the other guidance counsellor had just taken the grade 11 class on a field trip to University of British Columbia and then on another one to Simon Fraser University. This was meant to give us the flavour of each post-secondary institution, help us decide which way we might lean: toward fancy-assed doctor or sock-and-sandals social worker. Both schools looked like hell as far as I was concerned.

I figured there had to be other options. Even George's acting idea.

"The manager of our building is a drama coach," I told Sam as we walked in the mall. "He thinks I should be an actress."

Sam didn't answer, just kept those hard thin lips of his zipped tight. My mind flashed to his face the day he climbed Mel's front porch in Toronto, the way his mouth opened in shock when skinny Rick shoved him down the stairs. I felt bad for remembering.

"George said he doesn't usually let someone as young as me into his classes," I explained to Sam, "but he thinks I'm interesting. Like, *highly so.*" I wasn't going to take any damn class with George. I just wanted Sam to realize what a valuable asset I could be.

Before he could respond, a little kid started to scream just a few feet from us. His mother threw her cigarette on the floor and crushed it with her sneaker. The kid was down on the tiles now, wailing his head off, tears and snot all over his chubby red face. His mother bent over and grabbed him by the T-shirt. I remember the sight of her flesh bulging through her hot pink polyester stretch-pants, spilling over the elasticized waist. *Welfare pants,* I thought. Her blouse rode up as she jerked him onto his feet, smacked his butt and told him to knock it off. Welfare clothes, and welfare fat and welfare pissed-off. The kid choked it back, screamed some more and choked it back again.

I caught Sam's look of disgust before his eyes snapped away. He thinks that's us, I thought. Marlene and me. That's what he thinks. My face felt hot.

He walked faster toward Eaton's.

"Maybe you should learn a trade or somethin'," he said. "Or why don't you be a schoolteacher?" This from a man who referred to people with regular joe jobs as suckers. "I'm no sucker," Sam used to brag. "I don't carry a baloney bucket to work."

"Like you'd ever say that if I was a guy," I huffed. "God!" If I were a guy, Sam would teach me how to be a professional. I know he would. He said it before I was born. Then I turned out to be a girl. "How about I just throw in the towel and be a *nurse,*" I said to him.

Sam's face lit up a little, as if he was impressed that I might end up changing bedpans.

"1956 called," I muttered, "they want their *girlie* shit-jobs back."

No response from Sam.

In the accessories department of Eaton's, I picked four pairs of the priciest socks on the rack and then stomped into the lingerie department. Sam had it coming after that teacher crap. I made a show of holding up lacy black "panties" and he loitered in the aisle, with his back turned, hands jammed in his pockets.

After we left the mall, he took me home.

It's always awkward saying goodbye to Sam. He wouldn't come in, just sat there in the car, idling in front of our building. I gathered up the store bags and said thank you, told him I was sorry for getting cranky earlier.

He said he'd give me a call before he left town and gave me a stiff pat on the arm. "You just keep doin' good in school."

I nodded and got out of the car, and felt suddenly lonely. As if my father had just dropped me off at the side of the highway.

He waved. I did the same, turned and headed for the door.

I came into the apartment with masses of crunchy store bags. My Bonnie Tyler record was playing on the stereo.

"Sammie?" Marlene's voice was thin and startled. She came out of her cave of a bedroom with big black pupils, staring like a lemur.

Still in her nightie, a pair of my argyle knee socks bagged around her ankles. Two years ago, Marlene wouldn't have been caught dead in that getup. Then, somehow it got to be normal.

"*It's a heartache,*" Bonnie Tyler kept rasping. "*Nothing but a heartache.*"

Marlene stared at the shopping bags and turned back to her room.

"What's the matter?" I said.

No answer. I asked her again.

"I was scared he wouldn't bring you home, okay! You've been gone for hours."

"Where the hell was he going to take me?"

"Away. With him."

"Mom, I'm almost sixteen. A little large for kidnapping, don't you think?"

A strangled sort of snort came out of her. She slumped down on the edge of her bed.

"Can I turn this record off?" I said. "It's depressing."

"It's *your* record."

I shrugged, hauled my bags into her room and sat down beside her on the bed. "You wanna see what I got?"

Marlene watched as I pulled out each item. She fingered tops and T-shirts. She held the pantsuit jacket up to herself and looked in the mirror. I couldn't make out the expression on her face.

The next afternoon, I came home from school wearing my new bomber jacket and jeans. I was feeling stylish and expensive—the way Sam must feel every day. The apartment seemed dark and bleak, though, after I'd been out in the sunlight.

Marlene leaned in my door and watched me toss books on the bed. "You wear those goddamn jeans so tight—why didn't he buy you a coat that covers your ass?" Her *s*'s were sloppy.

I kicked off my new running shoes.

She chewed her cheek a second. "He just left."

"Dad? What was he doing here?"

"What do you think?" She blinked at the floor. "Compensation. Wasn't here five minutes before he started in." Marlene put on Sam's voice. "Come on, Momma." She mimed with her hands as though corralling livestock. "Pushing me into the bedroom. Come, on, Momma, come on . . . Nice guy, eh."

"What are you saying?"

She stood in my doorway and I sat on the bed and we stayed that way, staring, until her voice broke a little.

"I had to. He bought you all those clothes." She pushed her hair out of her eyes and then steadied herself on the door frame as she moved back into the hall. "Never mind. You're too young."

A minute later, the new top tore as I yanked it off. I swore and threw it on the floor. Marlene came back and asked what I was doing. She didn't look like she cared much.

I wanted to smash Sam's head into the sidewalk. "He *pushed* you? That's, like, *rape*."

"It wasn't rape. If he was with me, then he wasn't with *her,* was he." My mother's expression moved from slack to something like her old smugness for a second and then she went back to her room and closed the door.

———

Her meant Peggy, Sam's girlfriend. But I wonder now if it meant me too. Me and my bags of new clothes.

The kitchen sink is finally empty of dishes and I'm standing here with my hands in the dirty water, letting it drain, watching it swirl in circles and circles.

What's wrong with me? I'm just like them and I'm nothing like them.

When I was a kid, Marlene used to laugh at how easy it was to read my thoughts. "You ain't no poker-face, honey."

I used to picture an iron poker, the kind people use in a fireplace. I took it as a compliment.

I get it now, though. They can read me and I can't read them. I see what they want me to see. Although Marlene's no poker-face these days either. The only sharpy in this family now is Sam.

When you mark cards, you mark the flip side, the side the other players—the suckers—see, but only the hustler knows how to spot the marking. A good hustler can steer the game so that the cards go right where he wants them, but I'm no hustler. I'm a gold-plated sucker.

FIFTEEN

LOU IS DRIVING me in his huge black pickup to the road test centre. Three of us are in the cab, with Jill in the middle. The windows are open but she's still managing to stink up the joint with her perfume. Her hair seems particularly huge this afternoon.

Every morning after her shower, Jill sits at the kitchen table by the window and stares into one of those double-sided vanity mirrors. She sponges on foundation, and then powders herself from neckline to hairline before she brushes her cheeks with Winter Rose blusher. Next comes the Smoky Indigo eyeliner followed by two coats of Blackest Black mascara. Then she goes to work on her lips, making them shiny and purple. Once her face is on, she takes the towel off her wet head and plugs in her supersonic dryer. Holding it like a .44 Magnum, she blows sections of her hair over a round brush for about half an hour to give it "big curls and extra lift."

"I don't know how you can go through that blow-drying crap every single morning," I said once. "I just wash and go."

"That's because you're happy to go out looking like Cousin Itt," Jill said. "I have *style*."

Beside me now, her bangs spray over her forehead like a fountain. She's really jazzed about this whole driver's licence thing, cracking jokes and grinning her head off.

"You know how the test works, right?" she asks me. "It's a point system. So, if you run over a kid, it's ten points, old people are only five—"

"Jill," Lou warns her. "Give us some peace. Try and be supportive."

"I am supportive! I'm the cross-your-heart bra of friends. I lift, I separate . . ."

"Pipe down," Lou says as if he's completely exhausted.

I watch his giant hands on the wheel, steering his shiny monster though traffic. I can see why he prefers a vehicle like this: it probably feels normal to him to be seven feet higher than everyone else on the road.

Lou takes us down Willingdon Avenue and I try not to stare in the direction of Oak Shore Mental Health. But I feel a stab in my guts when I imagine her in there, sitting on the edge of her bed. Jill and Lou know she's in there too. If they're thinking about it, neither one lets on.

When we pull into the parking lot of the test centre, Jill gives me a big squeeze and a peck on the cheek and says, "Good luck, baby."

I wonder if she's left one of her purple lipstick prints on my face. She's as bad as my mother that way.

"You're going to do just fine," Lou assures me. "Jill told me you drove like an old pro the other night." His voice is especially low and quiet when he gives a compliment.

My face heats up.

"Pick you up at three-thirty," he says.

Jill grins and waves with both hands. "Make us proud, baby," she calls out the window.

The Young Drivers of Canada people have arranged for a test car to be here. I look around the lot and spot their logo on a white compact before I head inside.

The test centre has that cheap government-y feel and reminds me of the Social Services office, which makes me want to run. I force myself to walk tall and straight and I sit that way too when I fill out the form they give me. When I hand it back to the woman behind the counter, a wiry man with a craggy face peers over her shoulder at my form, and then looks up.

"You're my two-thirty," he says. "I'll meet you in the parking lot." He sounds like he gargles Drano and sand every night before bed.

Once we're both buckled into the test car, he sets the clipboard with my scoresheet in his lap and tells me that first we will do a pre-trip check. He gives me a minute to familiarize myself with the vehicle and then asks me to show him the left indicator, the right indicator, the high beams and the hand-brake. There's a kind of bored fatigue to the way he talks, as if assessing me is just one more in his long list of ass pains. He tells me to demonstrate my hand signals and all I want to do is flip him the bird, but I do the right thing.

Eventually he has me drive out onto Willingdon Avenue, change lanes and change back. I turn on the indicator and carefully check my mirrors and my blind spot both times. Just like in driver's ed. So far, so good.

He gets me to take the ramp onto Highway One, do some more lane changes and get off at the next exit. We drive up the steep hill on Boundary Road, the street that marks the division between Vancouver and Burnaby, and I imagine myself making a right turn and heading west, driving until I hit the beach, sand flying up from the back wheels.

Just before we reach Kingsway he gets me to hang a right onto a side street, then asks me to parallel park behind a blue Cadillac that is so clean and new, the glare off it is blinding. It's the flashiest car on the block. Why couldn't he pick an old beater for me to park behind?

Nerves are zipping through my guts and my face feels sunburned.

In order to parallel park I should pull up alongside the Cadillac and then back up slowly, turning the wheel toward the curb, but my brain keeps saying no, that I'll hit the perfect baby blue shininess of it and then some pissed-off rich bastard will come out of nowhere and beat the crap out of me. Actually, this car looks like the one Sam used to drive except Sam's was a two-tone.

As I ease into reverse, Sam's car keeps flashing through my head—royal and baby blue—and I can't help but steer away from the Caddy, pushing my car's back end back into the road.

"Oops. Sorry, that's not what I meant to do."

The assessor guy scribbles. "Try again," he says with his cranky toad delivery.

I put the car in reverse—and do the same thing all over again.

"Sorry. I'm just nervous."

He exhales through his nose and scribbles again. Did he just deduct points on *both* of my attempts?

He reaches over and pushes the car into park. "Think about what you're doing," he says. "Try again."

I flip my signal on, and reverse, telling the scared voice in my head to shut the fuck up. Sam is not here. And if he is, and I rip into his car, it serves him right.

I ease my foot off the brake, give it a little gas, and the car slips back alongside the curb just the way it's supposed to. The Cadillac's silver back bumper is directly in front of me now. It's perfect. I did it!

Why can't it be Sam's car in front of me? Why doesn't Sam come out of that white clapboard house over there and say, *Holy shit! That's my kid!*

The test guy doesn't remark. He doesn't scribble any more either, though.

"Pull up to the end of the block where there are no parked cars and make a three-point turn."

His voice really reminds me of Froggy from *The Little Rascals* show. Calm down, I think, he's just Froggy all grown up. Harmless.

I signal, carefully pull out, and head down the road, wondering why I'm such a jerk. Three tries, that took me. I *know* how to parallel park for fuck sakes. I know it. Froggy knows it. Sam would know it too if he took a friggin' look.

At the end of the block, I make a three-point turn. No mistakes.

Froggy has me drive us back out onto the main road and then up to Kingsway. You'd think I'd be nervous being on a busy street like Kingsway, but it's a relief after the parallel parking. All I have to do is stay in my own lane. Just watch the bumper in front of me like the driver's ed guy used to say: "Look in the direction you want to go and the car will follow."

We roll along, and for a minute or two I feel just the way Lou said, like an old pro. Even Froggy can see that I know what I'm doing now. It was only nerves back there.

He tells me to make a left turn at the next light and I sail into the intersection just as the light turns amber, and then effortlessly steer the car onto Willingdon Avenue again.

I am in the zone now. I am *acing* it.

"Why did you make that turn back there?"

I squeeze the steering wheel. "You said—"

"You should have *anticipated* that light would turn red. Should've stopped." He scribbles on his clipboard.

I don't get it. It's not illegal to turn left on an amber. Most of the time, that's what you *have* to do. Isn't it? I want to argue this point but I hear Marlene in my head: "You'd argue with your big toe if there was no one else in the room."

"At the next intersection, make a right-hand turn."

With the long line of traffic, it takes a while to make it to the corner. But when I do, I have just enough time to make a smooth right before the light changes and traffic starts coming from the other direction. It looks as if we're heading back to the test centre.

"Check your rear-view," he tells me.

"Okay. I did."

"Why do you think those cars are so close behind?"

I glance in the mirror again. "Because . . . because they're tailgating?"

"Try again."

My chest is starting to bang. "I'm going too slow?"

"Because you made that last turn just as eastbound traffic got a green light. You should have *anticipated* the light would turn and waited. Anticipate!"

Anticipate? I don't know what the hell he's talking about. *Anticipate*. If I could anticipate every friggin' thing that might happen, my life wouldn't be the bowl of turds that it is right now, would it.

My hands start to tremble and I grip the wheel harder.

At twenty past three, we drive back into the test centre parking lot. I put the car in park and pull on the emergency break.

Well, that's it. I failed. I suppose I have to take the whole damn test over again.

The test guy scribbles some more and circles something. He opens the clip on his board, and tears the top sheet off before he opens his door.

"Driving's not that hard, kid. *Practise. Anticipate.*" His voice is all snark—as if he thinks I'm some lowlife, a dirty little cockroach. That's what he thinks, I bet.

He tosses the scoresheet on the seat and slams the door behind him.

I pick up the paper. *Pass,* it says with a circle around it. I passed by one point.

I should be happy. But my throat hurts. Tears blur my vision. What a baby. What a goddamn baby I've turned into.

I open the car door and watch that cranky old reptile head back to the building. His thin, sinewy arm yanks open the door and he stands there, waiting for me.

SIXTEEN

WHEN LOU, JILL and I got back home, we told Ruby thàt I passed the driving test and she nearly wet her pants. She grabbed hold and gave me one of her octopus hugs before I could even finish my sentence. She's going to make me enjoy the hugging stuff if it kills her so I have resigned myself. Actually, I've discovered that when I relax—if Ruby feels tension, we'll be there all day—it's over quicker. I've also started to hug her right back. Good and hard. She giggles and squeals and lets me go.

Now we're sitting at the kitchen table. Just finished supper—spaghetti and meatballs—and Ruby sets a chocolate layer cake down in the middle of us. It says, *Congratulations, Sammie!* in red icing. There's a little Matchbox car on top: a red Mustang.

I stare at the cake now and I don't know what to say because it's just so goddamn nice of her. *What a classy thing to*

do—that's what Marlene would say. God, look at it! Two layers
and—and it's just so pretty and cute, the way the icing is, and
the little car and the chocolate, and the way my name has a big
exclamation point! My eyes are welling up again. Jesus, what's
wrong with me? I bawl when I'm sad and bawl when I'm happy.

"I waited for Lou's call before I finished the icing," Ruby
confesses.

"What if she'd flunked?" Jill wants to know.

"In that case, I thought I'd go with *At This Difficult Time,
Stuff Your Face.*"

"*Our Hearts Are Saddened,*" Jill suggests, "*But Our Bundt
Is With You.*"

Lou laughs. Me too. Feels good to be laughing. I'd told them
about Froggy, the test guy, at dinner and they'd cracked bad
frog jokes: *What's red and green and goes two hundred miles
an hour? A* road tester in a blender. *What kind of shoes do road
testers wear?* Open-toad sandals.

It cracks Ruby up every time I croak out, "*Anticipate!*"

Lou tells me I can borrow his truck whenever I need it.
"Same goes for Jill if she ever gets her licence," he says. He
forks some cake into his mouth.

"I have boobs," Jill says. "I don't have to drive."

Lou looks at his kid with dismay as he chews.

Jill giggles her ass off. "What, Daddy?"

"*What, Daddy?*" Ruby mimics. She's trying to savour the
sliver of cake she cut for herself. On the fridge there's a magnet
that reads, *A minute on the lips, a lifetime on the hips.* Another
one says, *Growling is your tummy's applause for a job well done!*

"I'm going to pretend you didn't say that," Lou says to Jill. "Your mother drive, Sammie?"

"Yup. She drives," I say.

"I don't enjoy it," Ruby says. "I'd rather Lou drove."

Marlene used to say that too. It used to bug her when Sam expected her to drive. She preferred to be "the lady," she said. This was back when we were a family. We used to go on these big road trips and stay in motels and hotels all over the United States. Sam said that south of the border there was ten times the money and ten times the suckers.

There was this one hustle called the Pigeon Drop where Marlene had to drive because of the character Sam liked to play. A good hustle is like a good movie: everyone's got a character to play and that's what makes the scene work. You can't break character either, from the time you arrive until you leave.

Marlene and Sam must have pulled this scam a ton of times but I can only remember the once. We were in the state of Florida, in the area where they keep Disney World. Marlene drove, Sam road shotgun, so to speak, and I sat in the back.

The set-up worked best in a busy shopping plaza with a bank. So that's where we were, window-shopping in some plaza in Orlando.

It was January and I was happy to be escaping winter and missing school. I think I was about six. Young enough that they didn't tell me much ahead of time; young enough that it didn't matter whether I had a poker-face or not.

Marlene had on a flamingo-pink pantsuit. She held my hand and I remember looking at her blonde ponytail and her thick bangs and thinking that she was the prettiest woman in the world.

"You look like TV," I told her. "Like *I Dream of Jeannie*."

She winked at me. Just like Jeannie would have.

I had a paper bag in my hand. That was my only job, to hold on to that paper bag and keep it shut.

We strolled along the plaza sidewalk, stopping at each window, peeking past the reflections into the shops. Sam dawdled, his jaws working, cheek muscles scrunched into the left side of his face. Marlene was still my mother, but Sam was playing my uncle now, my mother's brother. Sam loved to play a mentally retarded guy he called Farmer Lug. He *loved* spazzing the muscles in his face as if he had no control. He used to say, "If my face don't hurt afterward, I didn't do it right."

My mother and I were looking at a pair of Buster Browns in a shoe store when she turned her head. I followed her gaze to a bald man in a green sport coat who was walking in our direction. I used to wonder how she picked her suckers, but when I got older I *knew* who she would choose, by the way the guy moved, the way he dressed. This bald guy had a smarty-pants look on his face. He walked along in his green sport coat as though nobody in the world could look as good in that coat as he did. I felt the tension come into Marlene's hand. She turned from the shoe-store window and cleared her throat.

"Excuse me," Marlene said. "Do you know what time it is?"

His eyes slid over my mother's pantsuit, as if he wanted to swallow her. "Time to get a watch, sweetheart." He winked and then smiled as he glanced at his own. "It's twenty past one."

"Oh shoot. Thank you."

Marlene called to Sam in a sweet voice and told him that we had better hurry up.

The guy in green gave her another smile before he went on his way.

Pulling me by the hand, Marlene stepped off the curb as if we were heading for the car. I glanced back, looking for my father, and then stopped when he bent down to do up his shoelaces.

Sam let an envelope drop from under his arm and yelled, "What's this here?" as he picked it up. Gawking into his hands he turned in a circle, looking all around him. The man in green glanced back and paused.

Sam called out to him. "Hey! Mister, is this yours?" Sam opened the envelope. "Holy cow!"

The man turned and took a half-step toward Sam. "Whaddya got, pal?"

"Holyyyy . . . it's a million dollars . . . ha ha."

The man looked each of us up and down.

"There's nobody's name or no pictures," Sam said, his mouth ticking and twisting.

The faces he made! As if he was made out of Silly Putty. I started to laugh and my mother squeezed my hand.

"Honey, give me that." Next to Sam now, Marlene took the envelope. She counted the money inside—her lips moving so we could all see the total: *three thousand.*

The man in the green coat came a little closer. He was ours now: our big green pigeon.

I stayed close to my mother and held on to the paper lunch bag. I remember wondering if they were still alive in there. I brought the bag up to my ear and listened. The brown paper rattled suddenly as bugs batted the insides. I twitched my head away. They were so ugly—flying cockroaches. The thought of them crawling on my skin made me shiver.

"No ID or anything, huh?" the pigeon said, eyeing the money in my mother's hand.

"Nothing." Marlene stuffed it back in the envelope, as if the sight of all that cash made her nervous. "Oh, wait. Here's a little piece of paper. *Lucky Lady, 3–5; American Joy 5–7 . . . No winners.* I don't know what that means."

"Sounds like a bookie," the man told her.

"It's mine," Sam said and pulled it out of my mother's hands.

She took the envelope back from Sam. "Come on now, that doesn't belong to you. We have to find the rightful owner."

"It's mine!" Sam stomped. "I found it." He wrapped his arms around his head, pulling the kind of tantrum I'd have gotten a smack for.

"A bookie," the man repeated. "Loot he made taking bets. Dog racing, probably."

Marlene looked dubious.

The man's gaze dropped to the envelope. "Don't imagine that'd last too long in a lost and found."

"I expect not," she said. "I feel bad. This is a lot of money."

The man pushed his hands into his pockets. "Maybe it's our lucky day."

"It's our lucky day!" Sam shouted, and hugged himself.

"My name is Louise." Marlene offered the stranger her hand. "This is my brother, Teddy, and my little girl, Tina. We're not even from here. We're in town visiting my oldest brother."

"Orin." The man shook her hand. "I'm not from here either. Atlanta. Just here on business."

Marlene's eyes lit up as if she'd just stumbled on royalty. "An Atlanta businessman probably knows just what to do! I swear to God, as soon as I see cash, I get confused."

That's actually sort of true about her. When you work a hustle, it's good if you can incorporate your real self a bit. Within limits.

Orin started to shift around; he couldn't take his eyes off that envelope. "If you want my advice . . ."

"I would be *grateful*," Marlene said in that light smooth voice she used to be so good at. "Actually, you know what? My brother, Brian, is a lawyer. I should just call him. Maybe you could talk to him?" She started toward a phone booth. "He's right in town here."

Orin followed. "When you're dealing with cash—"

"It's my money!" Sam's tone see-sawed.

Marlene looked back. "If the people don't come back for their money then we'll split it. How does that sound? One thousand five hundred dollars just for you."

Sam clapped his hands.

My paper bag rattled a little and I flinched.

Waiting for my mother to put her call through, Orin smiled at me. "What you got in that bag, sweetie? I bet you've got some palmetto bugs."

"They're my pets," I said quietly. That was what Sam had told me when he gave me the bag.

On the phone, Marlene explained the situation. It was actually Fat Freddy at the other end, feeding her all the lines, my mother preparing him to talk to the pigeon should the pigeon insist.

"Brian," she said into the receiver, "we're leaving town, I don't have time for all that . . . Well, what's a *bond?* I don't understand what that means." She sighed as if she was exasperated. "Brian, why don't you explain it to Orin, the fellow who . . . *all right!* I'll try to do that . . . goodbye!"

She hung up the phone and turned to Orin. "He gets so *impatient.* He had a meeting to get to. Brian says to make it legal, we have to put up a bond for an equal amount and that we have to run an ad in the paper. If no one claims the money in thirty days, it's ours. Brian says he'll take care of the ad and he'll draw up the paperwork but we have to put the money in his safe if he handles it. What's a bond?"

Orin smiled patiently. "A bond is a kind of promissory agreement. When a bond is issued, there must be a deposit made and that insures both parties."

"Oh, honey, you're speaking Greek. I don't suppose you would be willing to take the money to my brother's office, would you? I promised my little one that I'd take her to Disney World and now everything's so complicated. I could give you whatever portion I owe for the bond and then if you could take care of the legal arrangements . . ."

"Sure!" Orin said. "Why don't we just nip into the bank here?"

She followed Orin into the bank, saying, "Will they cash my traveller's cheques?"

I looked up at Sam. "When are we going to Disney World?"

"She's gonna get me my money," he said, his face contorting. I wished he'd just talk normal for a second.

In a few minutes, my mother and the man came back out to the sidewalk and each of them had fifteen hundred dollars cash. Marlene slid hers into the envelope with the found money.

"What an ordeal!" she said as Orin handed her his. "Brian said we have to seal it, each of us signs it and then we put it in his safe. Here's his address." She handed Orin a business card.

This is the other important thing about these kinds of hustles: official-looking credentials. Fake business cards are good, brochures, fake personalized cheques—whatever it takes.

Marlene licked the bulging envelope and sealed it shut. "I'll just sign the flap. Um, where can I . . . ?" She giggled. "Can I use your back?"

Orin smiled. His face reddened and a trickle of sweat came down his temple. "When's your flight leave?" he asked as he turned his back to her. "Maybe I could take y'all for dinner."

"Aren't you sweet. That would be lovely! Why don't I take your card?" she said and set the envelope against his back.

Sam nudged me. "Wanna see her pets? She got pets!"

As Orin bent forward, I came under his nose and opened my paper bag. A couple dozen glistening thumb-sized bugs leapt and flew.

I dropped the bag and shrieked as they smacked against

my face and Orin's. Crawling on my forehead, in my hair. I screamed and spun in circles.

As Orin laughed and swiped the big bugs off our faces, my mother dropped the cash-fat envelope into her purse and pulled out a second identical envelope, which she'd already signed.

Sam cackled and smacked his thighs like a cartoon character. "Ha! She's crying! Big baby, big baby!"

I ran behind Marlene, batting my hair. "You're mean," I said to Sam. "I'm not your friend any more."

The idea that I would withhold my friendship always cracked Sam up. He laughed in character, though, and it gave me the creeps, as if his real self had gone away and wasn't coming back.

Once the bugs were gone, Orin turned and squared his back for Marlene again, still burping a few yucks as he caught his breath.

My mother signed the envelope. Then she turned and let Orin sign against her back. "My brother's office will be open till 6 p.m. Are you sure you don't mind doing this?"

"My pleasure," Orin said. He slipped the envelope she gave him into the inside breast pocket of his sport coat and then gave the pocket a pat as if to say *the cash is safe now*.

Later, looking out the back window of Sam's Cadillac, I waved to Orin as he stood in the parking lot and watched us drive away.

"Run away, you big green weasel, run away and steal all my loot," Marlene said into the rear-view mirror.

She didn't believe for a second that Orin would show up at the address on the business card she gave him. He was a bigger crook than all of us put together, the way she and Sam figured, and soon he would open the envelope and find nothing but a bunch of cut newspaper.

In the passenger side, my father's head lolled out the window. "So long, you big dummy," he said, Farmer Lug–style.

"Stop it!" I turned around to face my father. "You talk normal. Right now."

We had chocolate layer cake that night too. We picked up Fat Freddy at the motel and then Sam took us for dinner at a place that seemed very fancy to me. I wore a pink dress and black patent-leather shoes and Sam teased me with his half-wit voice all evening. I kicked him under the restaurant table, told him again that I wasn't his friend any more, and then he and Fat Freddy laughed themselves stupid. I couldn't figure out the joke.

Marlene told Freddy how brave I was. Freddy insisted I tell him the whole story, especially the part about the palmetto bugs—the flying cockroaches. "Were you scared? How big were they? Like this?" Freddy spread his palms a foot apart.

I brought his hands a little bit closer together and then explained how they got into my hair and on my face. Freddy shivered dramatically and told me that I deserved the biggest piece of chocolate cake in the restaurant. "Double-decker," he said, "with cherry filling!"

"How come she gets cake?" Sam asked Freddy. "She threw away all them pets I give her." He turned to me. "You even threw away Jerry. Jerry was the little guy with the hunting cap. He was a helluva nice bug, Jerry. He was married to Trudy, the one that had the blue shoes on."

Marlene giggled, and the more details Sam added, the harder she laughed. Sam grabbed her hand and kissed her knuckles. Freddy checked his watch.

"When are we going to Disney World?" I asked.

Before we moved on to the next town, Marlene and Sam took me, just like they had promised. All I remember about that day was being held in the arms of a giant mouse in red pants. I petted Mickey's fuzzy black arms and his snow-white gloves. Staring into the hard rubber smile, I thought I loved him.

That night Marlene said, "That crazy mouse didn't want to put you down. You nearly ran off with Mickey Mouse!" She gave me a big smack of a kiss. "I got you back, though. Promise you'll never leave me again? Promise!"

I promised. Never.

———

I look around the table tonight, as everyone is still yucking it up.

The chocolate cake is more than half gone. Ruby has snuck herself another skinny piece.

Jill has cracked another joke that I didn't catch, but I laugh anyway, just so that I don't look like the odd man out.

"Where did *you* just go?" Ruby asks me, smiling.

I shrug and smile back—give her lots of teeth. "Chocolate cake!" I say, as if that explains everything.

SEVENTEEN

RUBY GAVE ME five bucks for my allowance again this week. It's nice that she and Lou do that, but five bucks? What am I supposed to do with five bucks? Sam's word for money was *cush,* short for *cushion.* "Don't want to leave yourself without a little cush to fall back on."

Sucks not having any cush but I feel twitchy about pulling any more drugstore returns while I'm staying here. I feel like I'm being watched all the time. Jill likes to hang out with me and she's completely confounded if I take off on my own. She wants a reason.

Another support cheque came for me this morning. For Ruby and Lou, I mean. Ruby says it's a good thing, because she's never seen anyone pack it away like I do. She went bug-eyed a few minutes ago when she watched Jill and me making our sandwiches.

Jill's is regular peanut butter and jam. I started with peanut butter, sure, but then I felt creative: drizzled on chocolate sauce, sprinkled on some brown sugar, and a few dashes of cinnamon. Just as I was about to top it with the other piece of bread, I noticed a bag of marshmallows in the cupboard.

"Ew," Jill said as I sliced up a couple and added another layer to my masterpiece. She puffed her cheeks. "I think I'm going to boke."

"You better watch it, kiddo." Ruby gave me a backhand on the rump. "Keep eating like that and all you'll have left is your charm."

I bet she'd cram this whole mess into her gob in a heartbeat if nobody was watching.

Marlene has beefed up a bit in the last couple of years but she's never been what you'd call fat. And Sam has never been close to fat. (Although, one time the two of them were having a fight when I was a kid, and Marlene said to Sam, "You're nothing but a potbellied, little misery-guts." Sam couldn't answer—he just burst out laughing.)

Jill and I sit down at the kitchen table now with our sandwiches and Ruby joins us with a cup of coffee. I've got one of Jill's old sundresses on. The top is baggy but it's comfortable in this heat.

"Hey, um"—I take a bite of sandwich and chew as if it's a really casual question—"my dad never called here, did he?"

Ruby looks up. "No." She glances at Jill.

Jill shakes her head, and with a full mouth says, "*Mmffn.*"

"Are you expecting to hear from him?" Ruby asks.

"He's probably on the road. It's hard to get to a phone some-times when you're travelling. But he might be coming to town in the next little while so I just wondered."

"I always write down phone messages," Ruby says, and she gives me this sort of concerned look. She glances at my chest and then into her coffee cup. "You might want to do up those laces a little tighter," she says.

I glance down at the bodice of Jill's old dress. "Nothing much to cover." I laugh.

"They're going to hold a shuffleboard competition on Sammie's chest next weekend," Jill announces.

Ruby sips and glances at my chest again. Maybe it's bugging her that I don't wear a bra. I never wear one. I don't need one, and anyway, bras are totally uncomfortable.

"You should always pay attention to the way you dress," Ruby says, and looks me in the eye. "You want to look sexy-sweet not sexy-slut."

I start at the word *slut*.

Ruby stares into her coffee cup as if it's a crystal ball. "If you look slutty, Sammie, you could be the cause of another woman's rape."

I stare at her, speechless.

Beside me Jill nods. "Mm-hmm."

I glance sideways at Jill's boobs, which are pretty well burst-ing out of a low-cut white T-shirt.

"I've never even *kissed* anyone," I say. "How can I be a slut?"

"I didn't say you *are* a slut," Ruby clarifies.

"If you go around looking slutty," Jill explains, "you get a guy all worked up and he could take it out on someone else. Therefore, you could be the cause of some other girl's rape."

Ruby raises her gaze to the window and tilts her head as if Jill has just said something totally profound. "You might get attention by looking trashy," she says, "but be careful what you wish for."

I glance at Jill's cleavage again, take in her dark blue eyeliner and the stripy pink blusher on her cheeks and wonder if Ruby's actually talking to her daughter.

"The point I'm trying to make to you, Sammie," Ruby goes on, "is that it's easy to sit back and rely on your looks. You need to understand, though, that the most important thing for you to be is an interesting person. What you need to develop is a personality."

I blink into my peanut butter, brown sugar, chocolate and marshmallow sandwich, then I take a huge bite and chew for ages so that I can keep my mouth shut.

EIGHTEEN

SITTING NEAR THE back of the bus, I glance down the front of Jill's dress at my chest. I tie the bodice laces a little tighter and then glance around me. Nobody's looking. I'm not the cause of bugger-all.

Jill was peeved when I told her that I was taking off. But after that whole cause-of-another-chick's-rape thing, I'd rather listen to a dog fart than Jill talk.

"I just remembered it's Monday," I told her. "I have to go visit my mom."

Instead, I got on the bus and headed toward Vancouver. Just to move. Just to get the hell out of Burnaby.

Who does Ruby think she is? "Listen, you tubby little dyke," I imagine myself saying, "why don't you keep tabs on that cock-sucking virgin daughter of yours and leave me the fuck alone?"

An old man facing me on the other side of the bus recoils a little and I realize that I've been snarling for real. I try to look gentle for him, smiling and harmless, but he lowers his eyes and turns away as if I'm a hooligan.

I look down at my dress and loosen the laces again. Nobody gives a crap about my chest; they're all just staring out the nearest window. So I stare out my window too, and watch the stores fly past.

As the bus rolls through East Vancouver, I catch sight of a drugstore along Kingsway, nearly as big as a supermarket. I've been in that place before. A couple thousand people must go through that joint every day.

I ring the bell and get off at the next intersection.

Outside the drugstore, I surreptitiously check out the garbage can for an old receipt. Feels as if each person who comes in or out of the store doors gives me the once-over. My heart is a bird swooping around in my chest. I can see a receipt now but I can't bring myself to grab it. It's as if an alarm will be triggered—lights and bells will go off.

Sure, big words on the bus and now look at you. Some hustler you turned out to be.

I snatch it out of the can and march inside the store as if I'm late for an appointment. The total is thirty-two bucks and change: a hair dryer, a toothbrush and some shampoo.

A shopping basket with a discarded store bag sits a few feet inside the door and I grab it on my way.

There you go. You know what you're doing. You're Sam's girl, aren't you?

I drop the receipt into the basket so that I can read it without being too obvious. Down aisle 3, I grab the toothbrush. Two aisles over, I survey the shampoos while sliding the toothbrush inside the store bag. Just as I'm about to pick a bottle off the shelf, I catch sight of a guy a few feet over. He drops his head and looks down at the bottle in his hand.

Was he watching me just now? Did he see the toothbrush go into the bag? Wait a sec, was that guy just in the toothbrush section a minute ago?

I set the shampoo in the basket. He's busy with hair gel. He's not paying attention.

Hair gel? Seriously? He's only got about ten hairs on his head. Why is he looking at gel?

Don't be so friggin' paranoid. He's just a guy. Guys look. That's in their job description.

Over in the hair appliance aisle, I run my eyes over the wall of electric combs and blowers. When I spot the right model and price, I pause and look around: just a couple of women nearby but no shampoo guy.

I force my shoulders back and it feels as if my bones don't fit together properly.

Reaching for the box, I stop. Just past the end of the aisle, the balding shampoo guy walks by. The hair on my arms prickles. He pauses, lifts something off the shelf and then moves on.

My heart is banging around now but I set the blow-dryer box into my basket. Carefully. Quietly. Suddenly it seems important that I make no noise.

They say that breathing is the key to calm. So, I take

big snootfuls of air. *Slowly, slowly. No rush. Take it easy. No big deal.*

At the end of the aisle, directly in front of me, the shampoo guy walks by again.

My guts rumble and squeeze as if I have to go to the bathroom. I look behind me. Beside me. Jesus Christ. Don't know if I'm going crap myself or throw up.

See? See what living with these assholes has done to you? You're gutless, witless and broke. Suckhole! Baby!

I clench everything I have, my jaws, my arms, my butt, and head for the Customer Service and Returns desk.

Two people in line ahead of me.

Heat runs up and down my limbs. My skin is melting off.

Breathe through your nose, for chrissake! Breathe slow.

Finally it's my turn. I set my receipt and the box of blow-dryer, shampoo and toothbrush on the counter. The bag is in my hand.

"My mother bought this stuff yesterday," I say. "We don't need it." The words echo in my ears. Did I actually say that or did I just think it?

"My mother bought it," I try again. "We don't need it."

The clerk looks at me. "Okay." She picks up the receipt.

A hand lands on my shoulder. I flinch, jerk around.

Shampoo guy. Bald. There's a hard smirk on his face. "Can I talk to you for a sec?"

I look at the clerk. She looks from the bald guy back to me and doesn't say a word. I reach for the hair dryer.

"Leave it," he says.

The store tilts. I'm falling, pouring through the floor. The muck of me—jelly and blood and all of it turning inside out on the Tilt-A-Whirl floor.

He leads me by the elbow to the side of the counter. The colours of the drugstore spin. Blood roars in my ears.

He stares into my face. "What's your name?"

"What's your problem?"

He takes a plasticized ID out of his pocket. "Store detective," he says, and brings his face in close to mine. "You think I'm blind?"

"I never took anything!"

"Come on, kid. Seriously?" He still has my elbow.

"Prove it. I got a receipt!" I yank free. "You don't know anything." I bolt for the front doors, stumble out onto the sidewalk, and run.

Blocks and blocks. A car screeches to keep from hitting me in an intersection. I wish it had hit me. I go and go, panting and pumping hard. I wish something big and horrible would come down and crush me, just get it over with.

I am nearly back to Burnaby by the time I slow down. Wiping my face with the back of my hand, I look behind me. No one's coming. Everybody can see through me, though, into all the dark crannies and mucky, dirty holes. Everybody can see first-hand what a dirtbag I am, what a lowlife.

Ruby has the goods on me. Drew's mom too. Even Lou. Lou can see through my phony face; he can see that I don't deserve any of the nice things he ever said to me.

I miss Marlene. I just miss her so bad all of a sudden. I want her to squeeze me hard and say that I'm okay, that I'm good and smart and clean.

On the other side of Boundary Road, I fish around in my pocket for change and catch the next bus to Oak Shore Mental Health.

NINETEEN

"SHE SAID I need to get a personality."

"Leave it to a lard-arse like her to say an idiotic thing like that," Marlene says.

We're sitting in her room, each of us holding a cold can of Orange Crush that she bought us in the cafeteria.

"You have plenty of personality."

"I do!" I laugh my most incredulous laugh, the kind Marlene and I used to use when a really stupid actress was being interviewed on *The Merv Griffin Show*. I'm faking it, though. It's not that funny.

Marlene's pissed off and I'm glad of it. I feel mean and gristly when I think about what Ruby said, which is better than feeling small and shivery. I just sat there at the kitchen table like a little mute wart while Ruby spewed her crappy theories, even though I wanted to huck my plate through the window. In the end I went out and did something worse, though. More stupid. More useless. I haven't told Marlene. I can't.

"I do *not* like that woman," Marlene says now.

I look at the floor. That dark-in-my-guts feeling is coming back hard. Deceive, delude and desert: that's all I do these days. *Traitor.*

"I guess she's just trying to help me become a better person."

"A *better* person? So I raised a bad person? Is that where this is going?"

"No. I just mean that Ruby's usually all right. She made me a cake. I got my driver's licence, you know—so Ruby made me a chocolate congratulations cake."

"She's a bossy, abusive person. People like that are emotional bullies."

I roll that one around for a few seconds and wonder if it's a term they use here in group therapy. "She's not exactly a bully. She just has her ideas about certain things. I guess she's particular."

"Try peculiar."

I shrug.

"Now you're defending her."

I am, even though Marlene is saying what I wanted her to. What I thought I wanted to hear. I wish instead she'd hug me small again. Hug me quiet and soft.

She shakes her head. "I talked to Margaret, the social worker, because I was worried about our rent getting paid on time. Apparently that little *Ruby* actually tried to convince them not to give me my full cheque. *Ruby* wanted the Welfare to deduct the support that was going to her from *my cheque.*"

I study her face. "Why would a social worker tell you that?"

"Ha! I knew it." She looks defiant and victorious. As if she's just won big. "Margaret didn't spell it out in so many words. But I can put two and two together."

I focus on the top of my Orange Crush can, watch the little bubbles slide around in the rim, burst and liquefy. "Ruby figured you wouldn't need it since—"

"Who the hell is she to say what I need? You know what I remember most about her being in our place that day? The way she kept referring to you as *Sammie*. *Sammie* this and *Sammie* that. Like it was your name."

I glance up.

"Your name is *Samantha*. Sammie is what *I* call you."

I bullfrog my cheeks and exhale. I play with the pull-tab of my soda can. "She just wants me to feel like I'm part of the family, I guess."

"Well, you're not."

I'm the piggy in the middle right now. Marlene is jealous as hell and if I look at it from that angle, it feels kind of good.

"So when are they sending you home?"

Her eyes turn dark. They've probably been dark the whole time and I'm only noticing now how each black pupil is taking up her whole eyeball.

She glances out her door into the hall. "Wednesday, I think."

That's two days from now.

Sitting on her hands, Marlene kicks her feet out a little, looks at the toes of her shoes and then drags her heels back close.

"I washed the dishes," I say.

"What dishes? *Our* dishes? At the apartment? When?"

"Last week. Took down the garbage too."

"You did?" She looks baffled—as if I just said, *I painted the place plaid. Hope you like it.*

"Does that mean you're coming home?"

Now it's my turn to be scared. I don't want to go home with her. I don't want to live with her. Not yet. Maybe never.

"I didn't think so," Marlene says, and does that thing with her feet again. "That's okay. I quit drinking. And the pills too. Whether you come home or not. I'm quitting for myself."

I tuck my elbows in and wrap my fingers around the can in my hands, trying not to take up so much space. The walls still feel tight, though, tighter and tighter as if the box is shrinking, as if there's no room for me anywhere I go.

TWENTY

JILL ASKED PERMISSION for us to sleep outside in the old camper Lou and Ruby keep beside the house. Mostly it's just sleeping space, but there's also a tiny sink and a bathroom. Except that the water isn't hooked up. Drag. Still have to head into the house if we need to pee.

Jill said that sometimes they tow the camper to Vancouver Island or out to the Okanagan Valley. It's a bit musty but it smells like being away. Not that Sam and Marlene ever had a camper. That wasn't Sam's style. He'd rather stay in a hotel and skip out on the bill any day. As far as he was concerned that was the best way to keep the nut down. I wonder how he does it now. Everyone uses a credit card these days.

I wish I would quit thinking about that stuff. What's the likelihood that Sam and Marlene and I will ever be on the road together again? Zip.

I do like it out here in the camper. Especially now, when it's late. You can actually hear crickets.

"I bet it'll be great when it rains," I say to Jill as we're lying in the dark. "The sound of raindrops pelting the roof. Our own little house."

Jill is lying on the skinny bed on the left-hand side and I'm in the skinny bed on the right-hand side. I just said that thing about the rain to lighten the mood. A few minutes ago I'd asked Jill if she ever missed having a boyfriend, if she missed Roman, and it started to get weird.

"No way," Jill said. "It's summer. Having a boyfriend in summer is like bringing sand to the beach."

"Yeah!" I said and laughed.

It was quiet for a bit. I was thinking about how lame it is that I'm this old and I've never even kissed a guy.

"I don't think guys like me that way," I said.

No comment from Jill. It was embarrassing. Seemed like she didn't want to lie and didn't want to hurt my feelings either.

Then she said, "A couple days ago, my mom sat me down and told me that I should try not to be jealous of you." There was a long pause. Just as I was about to speak, she continued. "I was like, *jealous? Of her?* I mean, no offence, Sammie, but I never thought you were anything to write home about." Jill's voice had become mocking. Sort of like Crystal Norris's.

I stared up at the ceiling, let my eyes follow the cuts of street-light through the little camper curtains, the way it sliced the room into grey and black chunks.

Just as I was forming the question, Jill horned in with the answer.

"The reason she said it is that I told her how Crystal phoned me the other night. She said that Roman saw you and me out on the street somewhere and Roman wanted to know who you were and if you had a boyfriend. Obviously he's trying to make me jealous by saying that to Crystal, but when I told my mom I guess she was concerned that it could come between us."

"I'm not interested in Roman," I said.

Roman is this big Italian guy. He's got a soup-strainer of a moustache and a beak that hangs down over top of it. Jill used to joke that Roman's nose was roamin' all over his face. After school, I'd see her get into his ugly black Firebird with the huge flaming decal on the hood. They'd start necking and the tongue action was hard to stomach, but at the same time it was hard to look away. Sort of like when you see a dog throw up on the street.

"He's not your speed anyway," Jill said. Her voice was hard. "Roman is a total boob-man, so you'd have, like, *nada* to offer in that department."

"Totally!" I forced a laugh, looked through the space in the curtains and watched the moths flutter under the street lamp. That's when I said the thing about the rain, how cool it would be to hear the sound of raindrops pelting the roof.

"My mom thinks you and I should get a summer job," Jill suddenly says. "I think it's a good idea. You in?"

Probably the best part about being out here in the camper is the absence-of-Ruby aspect. But there's no real escape from her.

"I'm not sure," I say, nonchalant as I can be. "My dad's going to be coming out here soon. What if I have to go out of town? Because, you know, he was talking about me coming back to Toronto. With him. For a while."

"He was? When?"

"We're playing it by ear."

"What does he do again?"

"Huh?"

"For a living."

He's a rounder. I don't actually say that. God, I want to, though. I want to slam her right between the eyes with that one. "Do you know what a rounder is, Jill? Didn't think so. Not your speed really."

What I actually say is: "He's a salesman."

"What does he sell?"

"Oh, you name it. Cars, insurance, real estate . . ."

She's silent a few seconds, then says, "I don't want to be tied down either, you know. But I think we should accept responsibility for our finances and know what it means to earn our own money."

Clearly parroting Ruby with that last bit.

"Crystal's cousin works for Pacific Inn Catering," Jill continues. "They have the hotel restaurant but they also run a catering company for weddings and stuff. It's casual. You don't have to be somewhere *every day*—you just call in for work when you want it and they give you your hours."

"Maybe."

"It's good money. And it's almost August. Do you want the whole summer to go by and have nothing to show for it?"

God, I hate it when she sounds like her mother.

"Minimum wage isn't good money," I say.

"Minimum wage is $5.50. This pays $6. Plus tips. And you only work when you want to. Weekends mostly."

I'm no sucker, I can hear Sam say. *I don't carry a baloney bucket to work.*

What if he calls and asks me what I'm up to. I suppose I don't have to tell him that I'm waiting tables.

"Would I have to wear a hairnet?"

"No." Jill laughs. "We'd be working in banquet halls. Weddings and stuff. They wear a white nurse's uniform—those dress-things. It'll be cute. Mom says they have loads in second-hand stores so we could pick a couple up for next to nothing. Have you got a social insurance number?"

Is she kidding?

TWENTY-ONE

JILL TALKED ME into going with her to some government office this morning. We had to show our birth certificates and fill out forms and then they gave us each a social insurance number. Our permanent cards should come in the mail in the next couple of weeks.

Seems like every time I turn around, some government-type wants to suck out more information, assign me a number. I can't get past the sensation that every new number is like another crack in me, another way for the whole world to come seeping in. Marlene doesn't seem to care about this any more. Suddenly she's living in the nuthouse, gabbing with her social worker—*Margaret,* she called her the other day, as if they're best buds or something.

Before I left Oak Shore the last time, I noticed Marlene had an Alcoholics Anonymous pamphlet on her nightstand. I made a crack about it. She plucked up one labelled Alateen from underneath it and stuck it in my hand.

I let my lips move as I read. *Alateen is part of Al-Anon, which helps families and friends of alcoholics recover from the effects of living with the problem drinking of a relative or friend.*

"*Pass,*" I said. "I don't think I need to snivel to a roomful of dorks about my fucked-up childhood."

Marlene inhaled and released the breath slowly. "You were exposed to many things that you shouldn't have been exposed to," she said. "Much of that was my fault. I apologize for that."

I stared at her. "Oh really." I couldn't wait to see where this was going: A request to steal her some Valium? Get some cash together so we could have a fresh start? "And?"

"And you sound like you have some anger issues. Alateen might actually be a good thing for you."

Anger issues? I threw the Alateen pamphlet in the garbage can down the hall on the way out.

———

Jill and I are in side-by-side change rooms in a second-hand store.

Looking in the mirror, I do up the last buttons of a dowdy white uniform. It's Wednesday. Maybe Marlene's already been released. Maybe she's in her living room right now, sitting on the couch, staring at the walls. Maybe she's at an AA meeting spilling her guts. On the other hand, it wouldn't surprise me if she painted herself green again so she could stay a couple more weeks at Oak Shore.

Jill and I have filled out our applications at Pacific Inn Catering. They told us we could start this weekend if we wanted.

Jill said to me through the partition: "Wanna call in for hours when we get home?"

"*Want* is a strong word."

I tie the white cotton belt. I try pushing the knot to the side to see if I can make it look jaunty or something.

Fuck fuck fuck. Look at me—a pathetic little dishrag. If you had told me two years ago in the cab with Marlene—before we even got to Las Vegas—if you had said to me, "This is going to be the night that sends everything down the tubes," I wonder what I'd have done. Maybe I would have paid more attention to the little hairs standing up on my arms. Maybe I would have faked the whooping cough and said, *Forget it, I'm going home.* Vegas was the plan of someone who didn't have her head on straight. It was a new-low kind of hustle, but I didn't say so. Or maybe I did but I didn't say it with conviction.

"What's taking you?" Jill bellows. "Have you got it on?"

I pull the curtain aside and step out of my cubicle just as Jill steps out of hers. In front of the large mirror she tries to cinch her waist a little. The white cotton belt seems to sit right under her boobs. "Shit," she whispers. "I look like a big white maggot."

I raise one arm and check the tag dangling there. $4. "At least it's cheap."

She puts a hand on her hip. "Baby, I am a whole lotta woman. This uniform is not built for a body like mine."

"Mine neither."

Jill fidgets in the mirror. "Maybe if I put some darts in the waist."

"I deserve to look like a maggot—just more karma." I go back into my cubicle and drag the curtain closed behind me.

"What's that supposed to mean?"

"Nothing." I pull off the nurse dress.

———

Just before four o'clock Friday afternoon, Jill and I get off the bus outside the Pacific Inn. It's our first night on the job. They load us and three other staff into the white and blue catering van and haul us with the food to a banquet hall in East Vancouver.

Jill and I are both in uniform. Each of us has her hair pulled into a ponytail, though Jill has managed to tease out some big curls to frame her face and the usual geyser of bangs jets off her forehead. We've each been handed a bibbed apron to wear over top of the nurse outfit, which I like, because it looks sort of Amish, which means that I can imagine I'm Kelly McGillis in that movie *Witness*.

While the rest of the staff set up the chairs and unload chafing dishes, Jill and I are given a service lesson by a fussy little man who says his name is Hugh Tink. Hugh Tink is the team captain for tonight's service: a wedding reception for eighty.

"Knife on the right," he says. "Forks on the left, followed by the teaspoon and soup spoon." Then he moves on to the coffee cup, wineglass and water glass. When the place setting is down, he goes on to the next step. "To maintain uniform service, each of us must serve from the right and clear from the left. Understand?"

"Sure," Jill says.

"Repeat please," Hugh says.

"Excuse me?"

"How do we serve? Serve from the . . . ?"

"Left," Jill says. "And clear from the right."

"No." Hugh raises his finger straight up and down between his face and Jill's nose. "Serve *right,* clear *left.* If you serve them *right,* you can clear what's . . . ?"

"Left," we say in unison.

"Exactly. Remove dishes only when every guest at the table has finished eating. I'll leave you girls to it." He hurries back to the kitchen.

As the door swings shut behind him, Jill says, "Hugh T'ink he's gay?" and the two of us giggle uncontrollably. Mostly, I suppose, because we've already forgotten what Hugh said.

We study his place setting and duplicate his example in front of each chair, at each table, seventy-nine times.

———

By seven o'clock, a blister on my heel has bloomed, busted and bled all in the space of three hours because I forgot to wear socks and these stupid white sneakers I bought at the second-hand store don't fit properly.

Five minutes ago, the bride came barrelling into the kitchen with a cloudy-looking wineglass.

"Excuse me!" The hand that held the glass was inflamed, the skin cracking. There were scaly pink patches on her cheeks, and she'd covered a rash on her chin with chalky makeup that continued down onto her chest. She looked as if she wanted to beat someone's head in. "I mean, for pity's sake, it's filthy! Do I have to go through the whole place and inspect every glass? That is not my job. That is not my *job!*"

"Of course not, madam," Hugh Tink said. "This is *your* night." He gazed at her as if she was the most beautiful girl he'd ever seen.

"Well—well, maybe if you didn't hire children this wouldn't happen!" She waved her red cracking hand in my direction.

Hugh didn't need to turn his head. He knew who she was talking about. "This is Samantha's first night. But the rest of our staff are more than equipped to handle your every need. I assure you, you will see nothing but crystal-clear glass from here on in."

Once she had hauled her lacy white train back out the swinging kitchen door, Hugh Tink turned on Jill and me. "Did it not occur to you to inspect the glasses as you set each place?"

"I *looked*, Hugh. I honestly did." Jill's voice was suddenly thin and high. "I'm really sorry."

Hugh barely came up to Jill's chin. He turned to me.

I glanced at the kitchen door. "Well, it's not exactly screaming bright in there and my feet are blistered to hell."

Hugh glared. "There are Band-Aids in the first aid kit. Part of your job description is to own a pair of comfortable shoes." He walked away.

"Holy shit," Jill said. Blood from a burst blister had seeped pink through the back of my white canvas shoe. "*First aid!*" she hollered to the kitchen brigade. "Who's got the first aid kit?"

———

I'm all bandaged up, running back and forth from the banquet room to the kitchen. It's quarter past eight and we've begun clearing. Hugh has told me to keep away from the bride's side of the room. He wants the experienced "team members" to take care of the head table and, he said, he'd prefer she not be reminded of that spotty glass by catching sight of me.

I hate Hugh and I hate this hall and I really hate the *ping-ping-ping-ping* stuff. Every five minutes, we hear another jerk rapping his spoon against a wineglass, demanding the bride and groom kiss before he stands up and tells some boring, crappy story about their romance.

"She's going to punch your lights out if you don't stop staring," Jill says to me as we rush back into the kitchen with more armloads of mucky plates. "He's taken." She's talking about the groom.

"I'm just trying to figure out where I know him from."

"Sure, baby." She winks at me. "You gotta admit—he's cute."

I'm telling the truth, though. The bride is still miserable and rashy. The groom is tall and thin with blond hair and a pretty-boy face and he can't stop refilling his wineglass. Dinner's barely over and he nearly fell on his ass when he stood up for the last toast.

Once all the plates are cleared, and the chafing dishes are off the banquet tables, Hugh Tink wheels the wedding cake into the banquet room, followed by one of the other waiters carrying a tray of fruit, lemon tarts and Nanaimo bars.

My bandages are starting to work their way off my heels. One is sliding around my ankle; the other is slipping out the back of my shoe. "First-aid kit," I yell when I've scraped off the last plate.

The door swings behind Hugh as he comes back into the kitchen. He gives me a sour look. "For God's sake, Samantha, why are you barefoot in those sneakers? Wear hose and a decent pair of socks the next time you come to work and you'll save yourself a lot of heartache."

"For chrissake—" My mouth snaps shut.

Hugh looks at me, daring me to finish.

"I'm—I'm just trying to do a good job," I say. "And I'm *bleeding.*" Standing on one leg, I bend my knee, reach back and take hold of my most wounded foot.

Hugh looks at the blood on the canvas heel. "Take that out back and deal with it. I don't think the kitchen is really the place. Actually, just take your break now, please."

I hobble out back to the loading dock and sit down on the top step.

It's still light out. Staring down the potholed alley, I can see a scruffy bearded guy collecting bottles. I'd rather do what he's doing than this. Social insurance numbers are for suckers. The only people with social insurance numbers are the jerks who carry a baloney bucket to work.

It suddenly occurs to me that we're only about three blocks from Tenth Avenue Divine. Drew took me to Movie Night there once. They had their own projector and a screen set up in the sanctuary for the youth fellowship groups. The show was called *A Thief in the Night* and it was about this woman named Patty who wakes up and her husband is gone—his electric razor is still running in the sink. On the radio, the announcer says that millions of people around the world have suddenly disappeared the same way. Turns out the Rapture has happened and Patty was left behind when Jesus took all the real Christians up to heaven. The rest of the movie is about how Satanic forces now have control of the government and the people left behind must agree to receive a government number—666, the Mark of the Beast—or face the guillotine.

The soundtrack was cartoony and the actors sounded as if they were reading from a chalkboard. I started to snicker about ten minutes in. Drew gave me a soft elbow in the ribs, but soon he couldn't hold back the giggles either.

"Where did these dorks learn to act?" I whispered.

"The Academy of Wooden Indians," Drew said.

Mandy Peterson leaned over and hissed at us. "It's not about the acting, it's about the message."

"They should've stuck the message in a bottle," Drew said.

It was so bad even Mandy eventually lost it.

I miss that night right now. I miss it like a person. I wish that you could keep a certain day or night in your drawer and take it out every now and then and hold it up to your ear like a seashell. Or maybe I just miss Drew.

Inside the banquet hall, the deejay's voice comes over the speakers telling everyone to lend a hand and pull the tables back to make room for a dance floor. It's time for the first dance.

Some jerk starts banging his glass with a spoon again and then they all start up with the *ping-ping-ping-ping*. It sounds like a bunch of slot machines.

Big laughs follow.

I ease off my sneakers and cringe when behind me Lionel Richie and Diana Ross start into "Endless Love." Just when you think it can't get any worse.

I stare at the bloody mess of my heel and a flash of Marlene's bleeding face comes to me, her scared eyes crying, on her hands and knees in that Vegas hotel corridor.

Her poor goddamned face.

This shitty, stupid song. And the *ping-ping-ping-ping*. Like Vegas all over again. Sometimes I feel like a walking haunted house.

"Aren't you going to eat?"

I jerk around to see Jill standing behind me with a plate full of buffet food.

"I'm taking my break too," she says. "I got an extra piece of lasagna for you. There's hardly any leftovers, so if you're hungry you better get a plate or you'll be shit out of luck." She sits down beside me on the loading dock and dangles a slice of beef under my nose.

I wave it away.

She stuffs it into her mouth. Talking around it, she says, "I can't believe your friggin' feet." She chews some more and swallows.

I smooth new bandages onto my heels and rub the sticky parts against my skin, good and firm. The music from inside rolls on. Queen's "Crazy Little Thing Called Love" makes way for Cat Stevens' "Peace Train."

"*Folk* music?" Jill gags a little. "Play some *funk,* not folk. Play some Rick James, man, play some George Clinton. Who can dance to *this* shit?"

"I like this song." I pick up the extra fork she brought me and poke at the lasagna.

"You would," she says. "You and your little hippie blouses. All you need is some flowers in your hair and a joint in your mouth and you could get on that dance floor and twirl till you passed out."

"Cat Stevens is cool," I snap. I mean it too. When I was a kid I used to sing along like a maniac when Cat Stevens came on the radio singing "Wild World" or "Peace Train." He makes the kind of music that sounds like hope, even if it makes you cry.

"He's a Muslim," Jill says. "Packed it in and got himself a dozen wives."

"He did not. Shut up."

"You shut up. He did so, baby. I read it. He prays to Muhammad and shit now."

Gripping the wooden step with my toes, I sigh and look down the alley. "If your parents are Christian, how come they don't go to church?"

She shrugs. "We used to. Right around when they quit drinking. Christianity isn't just about the building, you know. Mom and Dad believe in Jesus, but church people can get majorly *pious*—wouldn't say shit if their mouth was full of it."

"So, Christian yes, church no."

"They just pray and try to do the right thing. I'm like that too. My mom thought it was a test of my convictions when Roman gave me an ultimatum and I kept my integrity. He can get bent as far as I'm concerned—because *I'm* still a virgin. I'm saving myself for Billy Dee Williams."

I snort.

She giggles.

"Do you believe in hell?" I ask her.

"Yup."

"Who do you think ends up there?"

"Why? You going to murder Hugh Tink?"

I look out to the main street and watch the cars pass. A couple walks down the slope of the sidewalk, the girl clipping along in purple suede platform boots and a dress that looks as if it's made out of a hundred ripped kerchiefs. She stops and cups her hands around her mouth, trying to light a cigarette. Her long blond Barbie hair whips in the breeze.

The guy brushes it out of her face. "You're going to set yourself on fire," I hear him say, and he laughs.

His voice gives me a jolt. I lean forward to get a better look.

"They're from the wedding party," Jill says. "He's okay. She's a hippie-dippy pain-in-the-ass. She probably requested this shitty song."

The wedding party? He's been here the whole time? Maybe I sensed that he was here and that's why he came into my mind. And who the hell is *she?*

I start to put one of my shoes back on but it hurts too much.

"How come you guys aren't in there doing the chicken dance?" Jill yells to them.

Big mouth. Jill and Ruby have the biggest mouths on the planet.

"You first," he calls back. He squints. Oh god. "Sammie?" He takes a couple of steps into the alley.

I give him a limp sort of wave. "Hey." My voice echoes high and squawky inside my skull.

"Holy shit, that's what's-his-face, isn't it—the guy who showed up at the door for you?" Jill hisses.

I nod, wish I could evaporate. Wish he'd come closer.

Drew looks back at the girl he's with. She's still on the corner, smoking. "It's Sammie," he says, and heads toward us.

"Who?" The blonde clomps down the alley after him.

"Hey, they're playing your song," he tells her.

"'Peace Train'?" she screams. "I'm missing my song!"

Jill nudges me with her foot.

Drew grins back at the girl, his noggin joggling around on his skinny neck like he's a bobble-head doll. His hands are like big bony puppy paws hanging out the sleeves of the jacket. Drew likes Cat Stevens. He played a mix tape he'd made when I was over at his house. There was Cat Stevens, Carole King and the Moody Blues and I loved all of it. Up in his bedroom, I watched Drew sing along to "Where Do the Children Play?" while we played checkers on his bed. His voice was so gentle and easy and I wanted to touch his hand so much. And then his mother came in to check on us again.

He stops at the bottom of the loading dock. "Hi," he says to me, his voice soft.

"What are you doing here?" And then he stuffs his hands into his pockets as if he just remembered how uncomfortable the situation is. "Are you guys waitresses for the reception?"

I nod. "First night on the job."

His blonde friend dances around in her purple platform heels and sings the last few notes of "Peace Train."

Jill scowls at her for a second and then displays my sneaker with the bloody heel for them. "Super-Waitress, here, forgot to wear socks."

"Sammie . . ." Drew looks as if it's his blood he's seeing.

The blonde stops swinging her flouncy kerchief dress and gawks at the shoe. "That's harsh," she says. "Man, I'd take the rest of the night off if I was you."

She looks as if she's our age. Maybe a year or two older.

"This is my cousin, Magnolia," Drew explains. "The one I told you about with the horses."

"*Maggie,*" she corrects him, and rolls her eyes. She's hanging on to the strap of a purple suede purse with fringes that dangle to the pavement.

Maggie. I remember him talking about some cousin who lived on a farm in Langley and wore see-through hippie tops with no bra. "It's hilarious when she's on one of the horses," he told me once. "Bouncing all over the place. And she's not flat either!"

People kiss their cousins. They marry them sometimes. I wonder what he's said to her about me. *Sammie? Oh, she's just some mixed-up jerk I used to hang around with.*

"The groom's my brother," Maggie says, her face incredulous. "He's the one who married that poor lady in the bridal gown. Did you catch her face? The entire experience has given her a rash."

Jill hoots as if she knows the whole family from way back. I chew my lips.

"Didn't you recognize him?" Drew asks me. "You met Shaye that time when we all went out on the boat. He was part of the College and Career group."

Now I remember him, stretched out, sunning himself on the bow of the boat with his best friend, Maurice. Pale and thin, Maurice kept his shirt on and wore his black hair slicked back in a sort of 1950s style. Maurice had a voice and a manner like Liberace and he was the femmiest guy I'd ever met. Though, I don't think I actually did meet him; he didn't talk much to anyone but Shaye.

"How come I haven't seen you all night?" Drew asks me.

"Because she pissed off the bride in the first ten minutes," Jill says. Loud. She's so damn loud. "She's supposed to stay away from her." Jill puts her dinner plate on my lap, takes a pack of smokes out of her purse and lights one.

"Ah, poor Trudy," Maggie says. "Don't take it personally. I'd be in a shitty mood if I had to marry into our family too."

Someone stomps out onto the loading dock behind us. I turn to see Hugh Tink standing there.

"You girls have about three more minutes," he says. "There are dessert plates to clear." He turns on his heel and goes back inside.

"Bag your face, motherfucker," Jill says once she's sure Hugh's out of earshot. "I just sat down!"

I reach for one of my sneakers again, undo the laces and spread the canvas as much as possible so that I don't rub my heel too much getting it in.

"Sammie," Drew says. "Don't. I—um—I got socks. Put mine on."

"Don't worry about it." I put my toes into the sneaker. "I'm fine."

"No." He sits on the step below me to undo his laces.

I look at his foot as he lifts it out of a black Oxford dress shoe. "Why are you wearing jock socks with a suit?"

"Because I'm a goof." He pulls one white tube sock off. "My mom just bought them for me. Brand new, see?" He takes off his other shoe and sock number two.

I can't look at Drew when he's this close. I stare at the socks in his hand instead. They look just like Ruby's chocolate layer cake to me right now. So damn nice.

I'm afraid to let my face move much because it feels as if chunks of me will start breaking off if I do.

"I didn't see your mom inside," I say, and the words come out all hoarse.

"Don't ask." He exhales.

"Big fight with *my* mom!" Maggie says from the bottom step. "Battle of the battleaxes."

I take my foot out of the sneaker while Drew slips his bare feet back into his dress shoes. He waves the socks in front of himself. "Lemme air 'em out a little for you."

Stop being so kind. Stop it, stop it, stop it!

Jill leans into my ear. "I'm going in. I'll tell Hugh you're in the bathroom." She takes a last drag off her cigarette, flicks it away and disappears inside.

"How's your mom?" Drew asks.

"Fine. Better. I don't know."

He lays one sock on his knee and then he gathers up the leg of the other and readies it for my foot as if I'm three years old.

I laugh a little. "I can put it on myself."

But I raise my foot and let him slip the cool damp cotton onto it. Setting my foot on his knee, he folds his white tube until it's an ankle sock. My eyes well up as he moves on to the second foot.

Maggie smiles as Drew carefully puts my shoes on. Her face is gentle and her big blue eyes remind me of a doll's.

"Better?" he asks me.

I nod and then whisper a thank you as I do up my laces. "I have to go back inside before I get in trouble."

The two of us stand up.

"Hey, Sammie," Maggie says. "You and Drew should come out to the farm and go riding this week."

Drew turns to me, his mouth opens a little, and I can hear him breathing.

"I have to go," I tell him, and start back up to the landing. "Thank you. And Maggie, too, um . . . nice to meet you."

Drew stands where he is, halfway down the steps. One pant leg rides up a bit and shows a sliver of his bare foot. It looks so vulnerable, like the soft spot on a baby's head.

I spend the rest of the night trying to stick with muck-work in the kitchen, scraping plates, dumping out chafing dishes, wrapping up leftovers.

Soon the music slows again. When the door swings open I see couples on the dance floor swaying to Bonnie Tyler's "Total Eclipse of the Heart." She sounds as if she's been crying all night and hasn't slept in days.

It's the slow songs that mess you up. It's the slowing down that gives your mind time to sink into a cold sad sea.

TWENTY-TWO

SATURDAY MORNING, I WAKE in the camper and the air is stifling. I move as quietly as I can, trying not to shake the whole thing as I step outside.

When I come into the house it feels quiet and empty.

I call out, "Hello!"

Silence. It's funny how you can always tell when there's someone in the house. Even if they're dead quiet or asleep somewhere, you feel it in your gut. Ruby and Lou are definitely not here.

One of the bandages from last night is flapping on my heel. I reach down and peel it off, stand on one foot so I can get a look at what's underneath: red circles of raw skin and scabbiness. Pink radiates out from the red and yellow foot-guts.

That dorky church movie flickers through my mind again: millions of people taken up in the Rapture. I'm glad I didn't see that movie when I was seven or eight years old; it would've scared the crap out of me. As it is, I'm imagining Drew and all the other good people thumbing a ride to heaven with Jesus. Everyone but me. And Jill—I just left Jill in the camper, out cold, arms framing her face like a pin-up girl. I've never known anyone who can sleep like Jill can: ten or eleven hours straight.

In the kitchen, the coffee pot is still warm and half full. I shuffle back to the front room and look out the window— Lou's big black truck is gone.

Back in the hall, I look at the phone, the pad of paper on the wall. *Gone to Safeway,* it says. *Mom and Dad.*

I wander into the bathroom to pee.

I don't know if I've ever been completely alone in this house. Sitting on the toilet, I gaze at the blue dolphins on the shower curtain—The phone rings sharp through the quiet and I jump.

It rings again. I look up at the crown moulding and consider whether Ruby and Lou actually own this place.

The phone rings a third time. I grab some TP and wonder how that must feel, owning your own house. Sam owns his own house. *Houses.*

Holy shit. What am I doing? That could be Sam.

I wipe and flush and haul up my pyjama pants as I go.

Rushing into the hallway, I grab the receiver off the wall. "Hello?"

The line clicks dead.

I hang up and stare at the phone, wait for the ringing to start up again.

I should just call. A normal daughter would call.

I pick up the receiver and run my dad's number in my head. I check my watch. Sam sleeps late. Sometimes he doesn't get in from work until five or six in the morning. It would be after 2 p.m. in Toronto, though. He'd be up.

When I was little, in the days before you could unplug your phone, Sam used to take the receiver off the hook and bury it under a mountain of pillows and blankets so that he wouldn't have to hear the crazy whining noise that phones make if the receiver gets knocked off for too long. I stand holding the phone so long that it actually starts up with that crazy whining noise. I push down the hook switch. When I get a dial tone again, I start dialling: 1–416 . . .

After four or five rings, someone picks up. There's rustling and then a sniffling. "Hello."

Shit. Peggy. She always sounds as if she's got a bad cold.

"Hi, um, this is Samantha. Is my dad home?"

"Oh." She pauses as if this is pretty strange that I should be calling her number. "Hello, Samantha. He's out of town, working."

I try to think of how to say this. "Well, um, well . . . I just wondered if you might have a number where he could be reached."

"What for?"

"To talk."

"Aren't you in Vancouver?"

"Yes."

"Well, that's where your dad is. I'm flying in to meet him tomorrow."

I stare at the pad of paper on the wall: *Gone to Safeway.* "Can I leave my number?"

She coughs as if her cold has turned into pneumonia and it's all my fault.

I read the number off the phone to her. My insides are winding tighter and tighter and I start to feel as if I might scream. I say, "Fat Freddy wants to get in touch about this thing of his. I have the details. Thanks. Bye." I hang up before she can say another word.

He'll have to call me now.

The phone rings. My skin jumps.

My hand hovers but I don't pick it up. What if it's Peggy again?

But it could be him.

Taking a big breath I clear my throat, clear out the gravel and the venom. "Hello?"

It's quiet on the other end.

"Dad?"

There's a *clunk* and *whirr* and then I hear a Fleetwood Mac song: Stevie Nicks singing "Storms."

Drew. This is Drew's music. On the day that he gave me the straw hat for my birthday, he also gave me a mix tape. He'd put all his favourite Fleetwood Mac songs on it: "Dreams," "Rhiannon," "Tusk." The song that was especially for me, he said, the one that made him think of me whenever he heard it was "Storms," because, he said, "You're always in storms."

I hug the receiver to me and let my forehead fall against the wall as I listen. In my ear, Stevie Nicks says she has never been a blue calm sea, she's always been a storm.

Where is my tape, the one that Drew made for me? I need to listen to the whole thing again and think of that day, sitting on the bench in Stanley Park together, eating cheeseburgers and drinking Orange Crush and listening to the tape on Drew's portable cassette player.

"Drew?" I say, as the song ends. "Can you hear me?"

There's some shuffling and then the *clunk* of the cassette player stopping. More shuffling and then the line goes dead. I put the phone back in its cradle. Maybe he didn't want to actually talk to me. Who could blame him?

At least he phoned. My own dad won't phone me. Drew keeps on being Drew, no matter what I do. And Sam keeps on being Sam.

I pick up the receiver again and stare at it a moment before I dial Drew's number. When he answers, I say, "Can't I hear you talk for a sec? Please? I mean . . . what I mean is, can I see you today?"

TWENTY-THREE

DREW AND I step off the bus in the middle of shit-kicking nowhere.

Across the two-lane highway, a half-dozen Holsteins munch grass in a wide flat field. Only a handful of houses are visible from where we stand and each of them is set way back, its own private little dirt road leading out to this half-assed highway we're on.

I watch the bus roll back onto the pavement and lumber away from us.

Drew inhales deeply.

"Smells like cow shit," I say.

"Seems like there's less *bull* shit out here, though." He laughs a little.

"Shouldn't've brought me if you didn't want bullshit." I laugh too and then stop short.

It feels crunchy between us. Took an hour to get here on the bus. I told him that I didn't bring his socks with me because I had to wash them first. Drew told me not to worry about it. That was the sum total of our conversation.

"Maggie's place is just over there," Drew says, and nods across the massive field behind us. We'll have to trudge another quarter-mile until we get to a smaller road, turn left and walk until we can't go any farther.

"Can't we cut across the field?"

"S'posed to be a bull in there."

All I see are two or three black and white cows spread out on acres of grass. No point in arguing, though. I follow him down the gravel shoulder. There are fresh bandages on my heels and my own thick socks in my old gym sneakers.

"She's going to think I'm a goof," I say, "for not having riding boots but—"

"I've just got running shoes on too, see—oh shit, your feet." He stops and looks down at my shoes. "The blisters. I wasn't thinking. It's almost a mile to Maggie's place."

"I'm fine."

He looks doubtful, but I start walking again so he does too.

We walk for about five minutes and the silence is killing me. Bits of last night flash through my head: Drew putting his socks on my feet; Maggie so golden-haired and serene at the foot of the stairs. *Battle of the battleaxes! Ha ha ha!*

"So . . ." I say, just as Drew says the same.

"Go 'head . . ."

"No, *you* go."

"When did you get that job at the banquet hall?"

"It's the catering company who hired me. Last night was my first—"

"Right, right. You said that. I forgot."

More silence. The gravel crunches under our feet. Then somewhere in the distance one of those cows gives a loud moan and another answers.

"*The cattle are lowing,*" I say.

"Huh?"

"Nothing."

I loved "Away in a Manger" when I was small. I really liked the part where it said that the cattle were *lowing*. It sounded cozy. You could almost smell the hay. I also liked the bits about the little Lord Jesus laying down his sweet head. And how the stars looked down where he lay asleep on the hay. All that stuff sounded like the best thing in the world when I was six or seven, even though I didn't really know who the hell the little Lord Jesus was. I figured his parents must have been rich people—a royal family who had recently lost everything. They were still kind and gentle, though, even now that they were all stuck sleeping in a barn. Even the cows and horses loved them and stayed close to keep them warm.

I don't tell Drew any of that. Used to be, when I remembered that kind of story, I'd say it right away and Drew would laugh and tell me some goofy thing that he used to believe when he was a little kid.

"Maggie seems nice," I try, finally. "Funny, I mean, and, um, down-to-earth. She's a real hippie-chick, huh?"

"Yeah, Maggie's cool. She can get along with *anybody*."

"'Battle of the battleaxes'!" I quote out loud. "So, was that, uh, how'd she—? What'd she mean? By that." Jesus, I can't even talk. I am the idiot child of Farmer Lug.

"It's stupid. Just my mother—She means my mother is friggin' *nosy*. Hey look, goats!" He points as we turn the corner and head down the narrow back road toward Maggie's farm.

Outside a beat-up shed, a kid head-butts his mother's backside and she turns around and bleats at him. Sounds as if she's laughing when she gives him a shove. The kid laughs along and comes back for more. Three or four more goats graze beyond them. Part of me wants to stay here, just sit on the fence and listen to these little goats *ha-ha-ha* at each other.

"Maggie's brother . . . Shaye doesn't live out here at the farm, you know," Drew says. "Even, like, before he got married. He had a place in town, down in the west end, with Maurice."

I nod.

"There was this sort of joke going around," Drew says, his voice suddenly tight, "or rumour or whatever, that Shaye and Maurice were boyfriends."

"Maurice is gay, right?"

"No!" Drew looks offended, which makes me want to disappear into the ditch. "He's a Christian. Shaye and Maurice are both Christians. So how can they be gay? That's not—"

"Can't you be into Jesus-stuff and be gay?"

"No! I mean, you could, but it's a sin. A major one. Like a—a hell sin, you know.".

I've never heard him so emphatic about the sin stuff.

"Anyway." Drew looks rattled now. "My *mother* gets into the fray and she starts calling Aunt Katy and saying that her and Uncle Ralph should get Shaye out of that apartment and into therapy. She actually started talking about kidnapping him and getting him deprogrammed. Like they do with the Moonies. I mean . . . Fuck!"

I flinch. It's not as if Drew never swears but it's kind of a big deal when he says *fuck*. Way more impressive than when I do it.

"Meanwhile, Shaye's dating *Trudy*. And Trudy, she goes to Broadway Tabernacle and those people are really, you know— those Broadway Tab people are hard-core! Trudy couldn't even say the word *gay*. The next thing you know, Shaye and Trudy are engaged and the plan is to get married right away, which, I admit, seems suspicious, but what do I know?"

"You think they rushed the wedding just to shut people up?"

"I don't know," he says. "And neither does my mother. She phones up Aunt Katy and this huge battle breaks out. And, of course, it all got back to Trudy and she got so freaked. Poor Trudy. She's really pretty but did you see her face last night? She's got a rash all over her cheeks right down onto her neck. It's all over her hands—she's covered in eczema or something. From the stress. In the end, my mother refused to go to the wedding because she's convinced that Shaye and Maurice have an 'unnatural' relationship. It's good she stayed the hell home, as far as I'm concerned, because it's none of her friggin' *business!*"

"Well, I hope Shaye's not gay," I say. "That'd be shitty for Trudy."

Drew stares at his feet as he walks. "He's not gay."

"Well, what if he is?"

"Then he should knock it off."

"What if he can't help it? Some babies are born with both sets of stuff, you know—like a hermaphrodite. What if a boy baby was born with a girl brain? He'd probably like guys. Then what?"

Drew starts to sputter and then says, "Well, if I had that problem then it'd be up to me to give what little I had to a woman. How can I be around Shaye if he's *gay?*"

"Because of sinning?"

He looks into my eyes for a second but doesn't say anything more.

"I didn't think you were so mean about sin."

I stop walking and look down into the ditch, and then out into the field at the one scruffy black and white cow grazing in the middle. It's a huge cow. *Huge.* It dawns on me that this must be the bull. I can see a slim wire fence now and realize that it separates him from a second cow. Another monster. I bet that second "she" is a he too.

Drew stops next to me. He jams his hands in his pockets and scrubs the gravel with his shoe.

"I don't feel good," I say.

Drew bounces his shoulders three or four times fast as if he's trying hard to shrug off the whole gay thing. He looks away, searching for words.

"Guess I just can't deal," he finally says. He keeps his face turned to the field, sucks in a nervous breath. "Are your feet hurting?"

No. My head is hurting. My heart is hurting. My whole life is hurting. If Drew knew who the hell I was, what my dad does, what my whole family is really like, he wouldn't be playing me Stevie Nicks songs, that's for damn sure.

"I don't know if I want to get on a horse today, to tell you the truth. I don't—I don't feel like making conversation with strangers right now."

He turns to me. "Maggie's not . . . Okay. We don't have to."

"I shouldn't have come out here. I only wanted to say thank you about the socks."

Drew nods.

"It's just that . . ." I look at the bull in the field. He's got no horns but I can see now that he's a bull all right. He looks harmless, though. Like Ferdinand. Suddenly I'm sure that something terrible will happen to that bull one day and I want to cry. "I'm sorry," I say. "That I've been such a shitty friend. You always do good-friend stuff. Like the socks last night. You're not mean, you're true—I mean real."

"I don't feel real. I feel like a total shit-heel."

We stand there together and watch the bull for another minute or two until I speak again. "They put my mom in some kind of mental institution."

Drew winces.

"Not like a *One Flew Over the Cuckoo's Nest* type of place. She could have gone home if she wanted to. Except she didn't. She did things, crazy shit, to make herself seem like she needed to be there. She didn't want to go home. I think she finally had to leave, though."

Drew stares into the ditch and then looks back the way we came. An eighteen-wheeler roars down the main highway, blasts his horn. A car coming from the opposite direction seems to disappear in the cloud of sand and dirt kicked up by the truck. Poor car. Poor bull. Poor everybody.

When it's quiet again, Drew says, "That night that your mom was at the police station, I meant what I said, you know. I wished I could have just driven you home with me and put you in my brother's old bed. I wished I had a quiet place just for you."

I shake my head. My eyes sting.

"Are you going to go back home with her or are you going to stay with Jill and her parents?"

"I thought my dad would come. I phoned him in Toronto and his girlfriend, Peggy, said he's here. In Vancouver."

Drew's hand brushes mine. His pinky grabs my pinky for a few seconds and then he takes my whole hand. It feels naked to me, my hand in his like this. As if all of my clothes have disappeared and I'm standing in the middle of Broadway.

He glances over his shoulder. "Come on," he whispers, and leads me across the road and up a grassy slope.

I can just see a big white house over the hill. It's set way back but this must be part of the same property. We sit down in the shade of a few trees.

Drew takes my hand with both of his now and holds it to his chest. There's a rush up and down me, as if cool air is zinging through my veins and into my brain. Part of me wants to pull my hand back, but if I do I might just float away, into the air like a helium balloon, fly into the sun and burst into shreds.

Then I burst anyway. "I mean, fucking Peggy—who the hell does she think she is? She was just some *booster* and now she acts like this. She used to be my mom's friend." Tears start down my face and no matter how hard I clench my jaws, I can't stop them. "I think my dad doesn't like me."

"Of course he does. He's your dad."

"Lots of people don't like their kids. His life has been way worse because of me."

"That's not true."

"You don't know me." I pull my hand away after all. "You don't know who I am. Or my dad. Or my mom. We're not nice—" I shut my eyes and mouth.

"I do so know you, Sammie. Just because I don't know every little—Who cares!"

"He's got good reason not to want to talk to me."

Drew fidgets with the grass in front of him, pulling out blades and twisting them together.

"Do you want to know or not?"

He nods.

If I tell this stuff to Drew now, I am the biggest traitor there ever was. But it's my goddamn story too.

TWENTY-FOUR

THIS STUFF HAPPENED ages ago, only a couple of months after the whole Mel debacle in Toronto. Drew doesn't know all the players and I find myself circling around and stuttering. I have to break it down, as if I'm speaking Latin, explain what it means when I say that Peggy is a booster, my father is a rounder and Fat Freddy is a fence.

Drew sits quietly, watching me. He looks so innocent and clean-cut and I'm embarrassed to be the one to explain this stuff to him.

I try to keep it simple, keep it to the story of how I single-handedly brought down the whole family. I tell Drew a bit about how Sam would stay out all night playing cards and Marlene would get so pissed off with him that she'd storm out of the house and stay out all night herself, just to get even. Like the time we ended up at Mel's place. But this particular time when Marlene took off, she actually had a legit excuse. She was in the hospital.

"What was wrong with her?" he asks.

"Female problems," I say. "Cysts on her womb."

At least that's how I remember it: Marlene explaining to me that she had this womb with lumps on it. Thing is, you recall an old story enough times, over enough years, and you start to wonder if you're making up the details that aren't there for you any more. Or were never there for you in the first place.

Whatever was wrong with her, Marlene had to be in the hospital for a few days. I was home alone one of those days, watching TV. I remember Bob Barker had just asked each contestant on *The Price Is Right* to guess the actual retail price of the lawn mower on stage. I remember because I guessed it exactly right—exactly!—and I wished someone had been there to witness my feat.

Just then, the front door opened and Sam and Fat Freddy banged into the front hall, hoisting a small sofa. They hustled it into the living room and set it down between me and *The Price Is Right*.

"Holy cow," I said. The sofa looked fancy and expensive: wine and cream-coloured upholstery, gold thread around the piping. "Is it a coming-home present for Mommy?"

"It's for you!" Sam lifted the cushions. The cushions were attached to the wood seat and the seat was actually the lid to a secret chamber. "Pretty cool hiding place, eh. Give her a try. See how you like it."

Climbing inside the pine box, I could have exploded from the thrill. "This is mine? Only mine?"

"Of course it's yours. You're my girl, aren'tcha!"

That same day, Sam and Freddy took me over to Freddy's place. I had never been to Freddy's before and my eyes nearly fell out of my head when I got a gander at his basement. It was like a cramped luxury department store. I was scared to move, afraid I might break something. I saw most of Freddy's inventory that afternoon, though, gold and crystal, fancy urns, Hummels and Royal Doulton figurines. Sam pushed all kinds of jewellery under my nose, chunky necklaces and fine bracelets, diamonds, jade and pearls. He detailed the difference between junk and gems and had me pay particular attention to one piece I would need to recall later.

He said he had a pal named John Reynolds. "John's that fella I played cards with the other night," he explained as though I'd been at the poker table with him. "How'd you like to help your old man play a trick on John? He's going to laugh, boy. He's going to get a real charge out of what you do."

"Me?"

"You got so smart studying all that game show stuff. Who else could do it but you! See, look, you'll climb right inside and then we'll put the lid down so it looks just like regular furniture. Then me and Freddy, we'll carry the sofa into his house, put you down in the fella's living room and you'll be hiding in there just like a secret present!"

I stared at him, excited. *Yes, yes, yes!* I wanted to help my old man. I wanted to be the one—the only one who could do it.

The next afternoon Sam and Freddy put on coveralls and loaded the sofa into the back of a cube truck. I rode inside the box, lounging on a furniture blanket, anticipating my big moment. Marlene's face flashed to mind, looking jealous. She always complained about being left home and here I was, going to work with Sam.

Sam needed *me*.

The brakes squealed as the truck stopped. I heard the back doors creak and open up. My belly did cartwheels when Sam lifted the lid and looked in at me.

"Should be just the fella's maid there this afternoon, okay?" he said. "Listen carefully. Wait till she goes upstairs. You have to be *real quiet*. There'll be the two statues in the den, remember the fat Buddha ones I showed you? Like them, except gold. They're heavy, so you take 'em one at a time. The other important thing is in the last bedroom down the hall. The jewellery box on the dresser. You take the whole thing. You got it?"

I nodded, though his words swirled in my head.

The sofa's lid came down and the pine box lurched as Freddy and Sam carried me toward the house.

The bell rang. Eventually the front door opened.

"We got a delivery here for Mr. Reynolds," Freddy said.

"I'm sorry but Mr. and Mrs. Reynolds are not in this afternoon." A woman's voice. I figured she was the maid.

"Uh-oh." This was Sam playing Farmer Lug. "Mr. Reynolds don't get his prize now."

Freddy interjected, "Ma'am, this is a gift from the Shriners for Mr. Reynolds's outstanding community service. Shipped in special from Italy. Just got to have you sign here and she's all yours."

It was quiet a moment. Then the maid said, "Nobody

called." She sighed. "All right. Where should I sign? . . . You can set it in that dining area."

The sofa lurched again as they carried it inside.

"Gee," Sam said. "This is the biggest house I ever saw!"

They set the sofa down. I was happy that the rocking stopped.

Sam started to hum, *"Tie a yellow ribbon round the old oak tree."* That song was a signal. Sam picked it because of how much I loved Tony Orlando and Dawn. When I heard "Tie a Yellow Ribbon," he said that would mean that everything was copasetic.

The maid thanked the men. The men thanked the maid. I heard a heavy door slam.

In the dark of the box, I fidgeted with the musty furniture blanket; the smell of wood was sour all of a sudden. The pine began to shrink and squeeze around me. I manoeuvred my back around splinters.

"Tie a yellow ribbon, hm hm hmm," the maid sang. I could hear her getting farther away, the creak of feet on stairs. I froze. My heart banged. I had not expected to be afraid. *This is my job,* I told myself. *Only I can do this job.* I wouldn't be the one left home alone. Sam would think I was a genius.

A vacuum started somewhere in the distance.

I inched the lid up and peered into the room. Slipping out, I crouched on the hardwood. Sam wasn't kidding. I had never been in a house so big, and with so many fancy things. Just like the home showcases on *The Price Is Right.* I caught sight of the two gold Buddhas. *The other important thing is in the last bedroom down the hall.*

I stared down the hall. Miles of shining hardwood floor.

Overhead, the ceiling creaked and my guts twisted. Looking back toward the Buddhas I noticed a ceramic lady in a red dress standing right between them. She was just like the Royal Doultons in Freddy's basement.

I tiptoed to the hutch where she stood. The figurine's honey hair was swept back and a white sash crossed her chest. I picked her up.

She looks just like Mommy, I thought.

I imagined giving her to my mother, presenting the lady like a prize when she came home from the hospital. The picture of my mother's thrilled smile was just forming in my head when the figurine fell through my hands and shattered on the hardwood floor.

The vacuum cleaner stopped.

I glanced up at the ceiling, turned too quickly and knocked another figurine onto the hardwood.

"Hello?" the maid called.

I reached for one of the gold statues. It took both hands just to drag it to the edge of the hutch. I tried to lift it off but it was so heavy I couldn't manage.

"Who's there?" the maid called.

Rushing back to the sofa, I fought with the lid.

The stairs creaked.

I climbed into the box. I lowered the lid.

Seconds later the lid rose again. The maid stared in.

I tried to remember what I was supposed to say if someone caught me: something about a cat. "I found John Doulton's cat . . . Mr. Royal's cat?"

"I think you better come out of there," the maid said. Her eyes were hard.

"My dad dropped me at the wrong house." It was the only thing I could think of—because it was supposed to happen like this: Sam and Freddy would ring the doorbell again. "There's been a mistake," they'd say. "This sofa has to go to a *James* Reynolds in Forest Hill." They would pick up the sofa and carry me away with all the fancy things I'd nabbed.

It didn't come off, though, and it was all because of me.

The maid ordered me to sit at the kitchen table, dialled the operator and asked for the police. Then she folded her arms and stared as we waited.

I started to cry. "I have to go. I need my daddy."

"The police will find your daddy," she said.

Outside, the squeal of the brakes: Sam's truck. I jumped up from the table and raced to the front door, beating the maid.

On the street out front, Sam was opening the back of the truck. He looked over his shoulder, saw me ripping out of the house and down the stairs.

I tripped off the last step and landed on the pavement. "Daddy!"

"Get in the fuckin' truck," Sam yelled.

Freddy dashed back to the passenger side. The maid ran past me down to the road.

Back in the driver's seat, my father turned the ignition. I screamed from where I lay there as the truck roared off down the tree-lined street.

The two cops who arrived minutes later asked me what my parents' names were.

I don't know, I said.

What's your phone number?

I don't know.

Where do you live?

I don't know.

When they put me in the back of the squad car, I panicked and told them my address. They drove me back to the house.

Sam and Freddy's truck was not out front and I was so relieved I thought I might wet my pants.

"Okay, then. Thank you for driving me," I said and reached for the door.

One of the cops gave a nasty chuckle. "Not so fast, kiddo."

"We're going to have to speak with your mother," the other said.

They tried the doorbell. No one answered.

There was a key to our front door hanging on a string around my neck but I kept it hidden under my clothes, afraid I'd get in big trouble if I let a couple of cops inside.

Finally I told them that Marlene was in the hospital. "She's sick. Maybe you could drop me off there," I suggested.

"What hospital?"

That one I really didn't know.

"Remember your mother's name yet?"

I started to cry.

Once I had confessed my mother's name, one of the cops went back to the squad car. From the porch, I watched him talk into a little black gizmo attached by a cord to the dashboard.

"What grade are you in, kiddo?" the cop beside me asked.

"I don't know," I said.

He huffed through his nose and glared down the road.

I watched the cop in the car some more and tried to think what to do. Eventually he returned to the steps and said that my mother had checked out of Toronto East General about two hours ago.

"See, she's coming home," I said. "She's on her way. Maybe in around ten minutes. I'll be fine here if you need to go."

The two cops and I sat on the front steps, waiting for my mother. It was nearly four in the afternoon when Marlene showed up. She got out of the cab and I watched her long slim legs, the high heels on her feet as she stood and stared up at the porch.

I rushed down the path toward her. Her nervous eyes darted to the police as she grabbed hold of me. "What the hell's going on," she whispered.

I couldn't speak.

She glanced behind her and down the road at the disappearing taxi.

The two cops followed us inside and stood in the front room while my mother sat on the couch and I slumped against her. The cops explained how they had found me.

"What do you mean he put her inside a sofa?" she asked. "No." She shook her head as if to make them take it back. "Jesus, Jesus, Jesus . . ." Her arms wrapped tight around me. "No one would do that. No one."

TWENTY-FIVE

DREW HAS LISTENED to the whole story without saying a word. When I finish, it's so quiet I feel like I'm suffocating.

Finally his hand reaches for mine and I let him take it. He squeezes softly and I squeeze back, a little scared— scared of what he must be thinking and scared that I might be struck by lightning for shooting off my mouth. When Sam and Marlene and I were all together, Marlene would call me Benedict Arnold if I told Sam something she believed was our secret. Maybe she was right. You don't go around knocking your crew or your family—even if it's just a little thing.

The two of us are staring down the slope toward the field where that big black-and-white bull munches the grass.

Finally Drew says, "I wish I could meet Sam in person. I'd like to punch him in the face."

I laugh nervously. He's holding my hand with both of his now as though it's a hurt bird.

"It's wrong what he did to you. You get that, don't you? You were a little girl."

"No, he—" I want to say something good about Sam but I can't think of anything at the moment.

"Yes," Drew says. "You were. He was supposed to look after you and be a dad. I don't know why you're such a good person after all that stuff, but you are. You're really good, Sammie." His voice breaks a little.

I can feel him looking at me and it takes all my guts to meet his gaze. He brings my fingers to his lips and kisses them. Then he reaches for my face and I am melting through the grass at his touch. He leans toward me and then he brings his mouth close to mine. Our foreheads knocks softy.

My heart starts to slam.

"I love you, Sammie, so much," he whispers.

He lets my hand go so that he can hold me with both arms. I hug back and it's as if I haven't been hugged for a thousand years.

"Me too," I whisper back.

He lifts his hands to my hair, then kisses my cheek, softly, and then again, and suddenly his mouth is on mine and he is kissing me for real, the way couples kiss. The way people kiss when they're in love.

We kiss and kiss and I'm shaking. Drew's whole self is shaking too and he's breathing as if he's in a panic. Except I think it's me who's panicked.

We lie back on the grass. He keeps kissing me, his hand moving on my back, kissing and kissing. Then his hand slides under my top. I don't wear a bra. His hand is on my back, right on my bare skin.

"Don't," I whisper.

I reach to push his hand off my back but he fumbles it around to my side and runs it over my ribs. I tuck my elbows in close.

"Drew," I whisper.

His hand comes round onto my stomach, though, and then higher. He's kissing and kissing me, kissing my neck. Then he's touching my breast.

"Don't!" I push him hard. "What are you *doing?*"

He sits up. "What? I'm sorry. I didn't mean—I just."

"I thought you said you *loved* me." I yank my top back down over my stomach.

"I do. I—"

"Then, why are you trying to—?"

"I wasn't!" His knees are up and his arms are wrapped around them now. "Sammie, I didn't mean to. I just—I was touching you because I thought—"

"You thought what?" My knees are up too now. "You thought I was like *her?*"

"Who?"

"I'm *not.* I'm nothing like her. And I'm nothing like him."

He looks at me, then looks away. "I know," he says.

I hold my knees crushed to my chest. His hand was right *there.* The sensation won't stop and I try to rub it off against my legs.

We sit that way for a while not saying a thing. Drew and I are sitting six inches apart and it's the loneliest I've ever felt. The night Drew took me to pick up Marlene in jail flashes to mind—me alone in the hall when it was all over. This feels worse than that.

"I have to go," I say.

He looks at me, his eyes red and watery. He nods.

———

We walk back to the bus stop. Drew keeps his hands in his pockets. I walk with my arms crossed and my head down as if it's the middle of winter.

On the bus, we don't speak all the way into town. I stare out the window and Drew looks at his lap.

When we get to the bus loop in Vancouver, his bus is already there. He's going to head back to his family's snazzy hilltop house in North Burnaby and I'm going back to Jill's place.

"I'll wait with you," he says quietly.

"You don't have to."

"I want to."

It's only a few minutes until my bus rolls into the loop and pulls up in front of us. Drew meets my eyes and then stares down at the pavement.

"Please don't disappear," he says. "I'm sorry. I'll never do anything like that again."

Marlene's voice echoes in my mind: *He's a doll. You should marry him.*

I'm ready to start bawling all over. I can't uncross my arms. At the same time, I almost wish Drew could hide me inside his coat and sneak me home with him, hold my two hands and look into my eyes the way he did before everything went haywire back there in Langley.

He puts a hand on my arm and I manage to open my arms up and we give each other a stiff sort of hug.

"Sammie? Aren't we okay? Please?"

"Okay," I say. "Yeah. Yes."

The bus's engine rumbles a little louder as the driver gets ready to leave and Drew and I let each other go. He watches as I run to get on board.

Sitting by a window, I mouth *goodbye* to him as we head out. He waves back, and stuffs his hands back into his pockets. His smile is weak and his eyes are still swollen.

Just before we turn a corner, I glance back, but I can't see him. Can't see the bus loop at all. And now that I can't, there's an empty dark room in my guts. He'd like to punch Sam in the face, he said.

But I hid in the sofa. I knew what I was there for. It's true that Sam tried to tell me that it was just a game, but that's what dads do with little kids. That's how you make work seem fun.

I shouldn't have knocked Sam to Drew, but it hurts like hell that Sam doesn't call me. Maybe all I wanted was for someone else to be the asshole for a few minutes. But that's what a phony does: he rats out the other guy and then makes like he's just an innocent.

I've always felt shitty about that sofa story. Sam tried to

include me in a sure thing and I made a hash of it, breaking things, stumbling around—I didn't even have the sense to boost the stuff I was sent for. John Reynolds, the mark, likely had it coming. He probably tried to sneak a cooler into Sam's poker game and then refused to cop to it. Why blame Sam for wanting to get his money back?

Staring out the window, watching the buildings swipe past, I imagine Drew as he arrives home, walking past his father's shiny car in the driveway, coming through the front door of that big clean house. Drew's bedroom is at the very top. It's almost an attic: wooden beams cut across the ceiling—rich, dark, beat-up wood, like people with money always seem to have—and there's a big picture window. It's a real guy's bedroom: his older brother's model cars are on the shelves and he has a ship-in-a-bottle that his grandfather made.

I picture him walking through the house now and going straight up to that bedroom of his. I can see him looking out the window at his fresh view of the water and the mountains. Everything around him is sweet and rich and homey. In the midst of all that, if Drew thinks of me, the things I told him about my family, touching me and being touched by my skeevy little world—I bet he'll want to shower and wash me off.

Sam used to say, "Not much about a rounder squares with a square john." What he meant was that, most of the time, straight people just don't get it. Marlene, Sam and me—and Freddy too—we don't think like regular people. After that sofa hustle, the cops picked up Sam and Freddy and threw them in the can. The two of them did almost two years.

Marlene packed the two of us up and moved back to Vancouver. The fall I started grade 5, though, I heard my mother on the phone in her bedroom, honey-voiced, a little giggly when she said, "Boy oh boy, some friend you are." The tone of her voice made a little part of me pop like a firecracker, hoping to hell it was Sam at the other end of the line.

I loitered around her bedroom door, trying to hear. The second my mother hung up, I plagued her with questions.

Turned out it was Fat Freddy on the phone. He was out of the joint early: a free man.

"What about dad? Where's dad?"

"Supposedly they're not in touch—Freddy's moved out here now." She rolled her eyes a little, her mouth flirtatious. "*Come on, Leni,*" she imitated a whiny, needy Freddy. "*Let's have dinner.*"

Two days later, Freddy called again. He had done a little investigating and discovered that Sam was out and shacked up with Peggy in Toronto. My mother's friend, Peggy. Peggy, the booster. Freddy then proceeded to invite himself over to our place for a drink. Marlene hung up in his ear. She was spitting fire for weeks. You can bet she lit into Sam when he finally got around to calling her.

Regular people wouldn't even be speaking to each other after all that's happened with us. But a rounder has got to make a living. It sounds ruthless. And sometimes it is. Actually, most of the time, the life of a hustler is pretty much the same as the one that regular people live. Straight people don't like to admit it but they work with jerks they don't like and they sell situations they don't believe in every day to make a buck. If you step back and squint you realize that most legit businesses are working a hustle too. Go into a supermarket and they'll sell you a bottle of water for a whole dollar when all you have to do is go home and turn on the tap for free. Stick the word *France* on the label and the suckers'll line up and pay double! And what about the banks? They take all your cash and charge you for it every time you ask for a little back. They get you to use their credit cards and then make you pay them twenty percent interest. You pay if it's your money and you pay if it's their money. If that's not crooked, I don't know what is. That's as good as loan sharking. Sam doesn't even have a bank account. Marlene says he's a dope on that count and that sending cash through the mail is moronic. But I think he's got a point. Pay cash and keep the rest.

The bus is muggy with the day's stale heat. The month of August always sounds so warm and dreamy when you're stuck in February but once you're actually here, right in the midst of worn, old August heat, all you can think about is the fact that September is coming. In the past, I've always dreaded the new school year: classes I didn't want to sit through, schedules I didn't want to keep. Sitting here on this overripe bus, *September* sounds like a foreign word. What does September mean for Marlene? Or me? Or Sam for that matter?

He's here, though. Sam could be in any of these buildings, on any one of these streets.

I wish I could meet Sam in person. I'd like to punch him in the face.

As we turn up Willingdon Avenue, I feel queasy. Maybe just carsick from riding a bus all over hell's half acre. I don't think that's it, though. I'm a creep, that's what it is. I'm a creep and it's making me sick.

I'm the one who deserves a punch. I didn't tell Drew about my drugstore returns, did I. I didn't tell him about how screaming-good it can be, how when a hustle's going right it makes your blood sing through your wrists—the way it feels as if your hair is standing straight on end when you walk away scot-free with a pocket full of cash.

And here's another thing I left out: I *want* Sam to come and get me. I want Sam to drive up in front of Jill's place and say, "Forget your bags, we'll buy you clothes along the way. Just get in, sweetheart!"

The best September I can think of would be sitting in the passenger seat next to my dad, driving south, working every angle we can, taking every sucker, from here straight on down the west coast—Seattle, San Francisco, Los Angeles, San Diego—milking them dry before they know what hit 'em. Then we'd head east, right across to Florida and all the way up to New York City! I'd be there by his side, proving that I really am Sam's girl.

I am not the loser in the drugstore, the girl who freaks out when some two-bit rent-a-cop says *boo.*

I am not the sucker in the nurse's uniform and catering apron, covered in other people's slop.

Drew's mother had my number from the second she laid eyes on me. If Drew could read my mind like she can, see my two faces, my itch to be with Sam, he'd know she was right.

Why can't Sam just call me and tell me the score? Tell me what the hell's going on?

The bus reaches the top of Willingdon Avenue and the driver is about to head east on Kingsway. But I'm not ready to go back to Jill's yet. I can't *stand* it. All of a sudden, I can't stand the thought of anybody who isn't us. I'm not Jill and I'm not Ruby and I'm not Drew either. I am Sam's girl. I am Marlene's.

I need air.

I reach and ring the bell.

On the sidewalk, I gulp the warmed-over traffic breeze, catch a green light and race across the street. I start heading the wrong way down Kingsway, west, past Old Orchard Mall, jogging. I'm not sure if I'm running from something or running to it.

When I'm out of breath I turn to walk down Sardis, our little side street. It's not such a bad street. The breeze is picking up, fluttering the leaves overhead, ruffling my hair as it goes, whispering against my ears. I listen to the rustle in the trees and think about the way it sounds serene and restless all at once.

The geraniums in front of the apartment building are fire bright against the dark earth. Why can't I just appreciate the things that are good? Fine, it's not fancy around here, it's not downtown, but it's not horrible.

I step off the sidewalk onto the dirt and wood-chips of the building's back garden and try to see into our apartment in the corner. It's hard to make out the ordinary dim of the indoors when the hard gold of the setting sun is blasting the window, obliterating everything.

I keep behind the pine trees at the rear of our building. I just want to see if she's in there. If she came home.

A hand reaches out through the curtain and I tense as it pushes the window farther open. Then the sliding door to the balcony grumbles sideways on its runners. And suddenly there's Marlene.

Stepping outside, she looks unsteady, as if she's not used to the outdoors, the bright light. As if she's on fawn legs.

She cups her hand over her eyes. She's looking up. I stare up too, at the sky, and see that it's the crows she's watching. The sky is teeming with black birds heading east for the night.

Every night around sunset the crows leave Vancouver and head out here to Burnaby. They've always done it, ever since I can remember. It gave me the willies when I was little, like something from an Alfred Hitchcock movie. But now I like it. I like the idea of all those birds moving together when it's time for bed, flying east, away from the setting sun, as if they've got to get tucked in before the lights go out.

Looking down again, Marlene takes a step farther onto the balcony, sets both her hands on the metal railing and her sights straight back toward the alley as if she's studying the bushes. She tips her head back once more, and closes her eyes to the sun for a moment. She looks so pretty that I flash back to that day in Orlando: the prettiest woman in the world. Marlene in her flamingo-pink pantsuit, holding my hand.

She leans on the railing for a few seconds, light shining on her blonde hair. I wish I could touch it, the gold of it, but I stand here like a ghost, shielded by the screaming brilliance of the setting sun.

After a little while, my mother lowers her chin and glances toward the sliding door into the apartment. She looks reluctant, as though a prison guard is calling her back to a cell, but she goes.

I watch her disappear inside and then I turn and go too, back in the direction I came from.

TWENTY-SIX

IT'S A LITTLE before nine when I come into the house. Almost dark outside. Ruby and Lou are on the couch in front of the television. There's a giant bowl of popcorn between them.

"Aha! The mystery woman returns," Lou says.

"Jill left for a party about twenty minutes ago," Ruby tells me. "She wanted you to come along but she didn't know how to get hold of you."

"That's okay. I'm tired anyway."

"Did you go horseback riding?" Lou asks.

"Na, we just walked around and looked at cows."

Ruby laughs hard at that one. I don't know why. She does that sometimes.

They seem so cozy together, Ruby and Lou, that I'm not sure where to look.

"Pull up a chair and stay a while," Ruby says.

I sit down on the second couch.

"You're just in time to watch *The Way We Were*," Lou says. "Want some popcorn? Here, let me get you a bowl."

Ruby steadies the big bowl beside her as Lou gets up.

"You look like you got a little colour today," she says.

"Probably." I rub my eyes. They feel as if they're full of sand after all that time in the sun.

"I talked to your mother a little while ago."

I blink at her and keep my mouth shut. The television splashes blue light on Ruby's face.

"I didn't call her. She called *me*," Ruby says as if she can read my mind.

Marlene called Ruby? I wonder if she saw me sneaking around out back.

Lou returns from the kitchen with a smaller version of the bowl on the couch. He shoves a bunch of popcorn into it and then hands it to me before he sits and licks butter and salt off his fingers.

"She really misses you, Sammie," Ruby says. "She quit drinking, she told me, and she's in AA. She sounds pretty damn good, considering. Except that she hasn't talked to *you* in a while."

I don't know what to say to that.

"She'd like to see you."

I glance out the window into the blue dusk.

"Don't you think you should go and see her soon?"

Lou keeps his eyes on the television.

I nod.

"What are your plans, Sammie? What do you think about September?" Ruby asks.

I look at her.

"Your mom's doing a lot better. If she keeps it up, you'll be going home soon."

I turn my face to the TV. Robert Redford is jogging through the park right past Barbara Streisand.

"It's started!" Ruby yelps as the piano starts to plink out the theme and Streisand hums along. "Turn it up, Lou."

She braces the bowl once more as Lou jumps up and turns the volume knob on the television.

"*Memories* . . ." Streisand sings. They light the corners of her mind.

Another wrist-slasher of a song. Right up there with "Theme from Mahogany." I stuff popcorn into my mouth.

My eyes drift to Ruby and Lou cuddled together on the couch. Lou's got his arm around her, and she's got her head nestled into his shoulder. What must it feel like to be Ruby, to have Lou watching out for you all the time? A person wouldn't have to be so careful, wouldn't have to keep their antennae so pricked. I imagine myself snuggled against Lou's arm. You wouldn't have to be big around Lou; you could afford to just let yourself be small.

———

It's about two in the morning now and I still can't sleep. Jill's not back. Maybe she called home after I went to bed. Probably staying over at Crystal's house.

I barely heard a word of that sappy movie tonight. Ruby snivelled all over the place and went through half a box of Kleenex. Not me. I was too busy thinking about Drew assuming he could just touch me like that. I can't figure out if I'm being childish. I don't even have someone I can talk to about it. Definitely not Ruby.

Ruby is not my mother. These people are not my family.

Drew is not my family either.

Lying in bed, I stare at the ceiling. Outside, headlights come down the road and light up the camper curtain for a second or two. Brakes squeak. There is a pause and then I hear a car door open and slam shut.

The camper door creaks and Jill climbs in, shaking the whole frame. I squint at my watch, trying to make out the actual time.

"Hi," I whisper.

She sniffles.

"Jill?"

No response. I watch her silhouette as she takes off her leather jacket.

"What's the matter?"

"Go to sleep." Her voice is warbly. She unzips her jeans and wriggles out of them, shaking the trailer some more as she sits on her bed. She pulls back the covers and crawls under them. "Where the hell were *you* all goddamn day?"

The booze smell coming off her is sour, as if she's been drinking all night and it's making its way out of her pores now.

"I told you. I went out to Langley with Drew."

Silence.

"Where were *you* tonight?"

"Making a fucking ass of myself," she says.

"Oh yeah? Right on." I'm trying to be light, make fun of what likely isn't a very big deal. "Where?"

"Byrne Road."

Another bush party. She tells me she got a call about it from Mark, one of the guys from her regular crowd at school. When she couldn't get hold of Crystal, she called Mark back and caught a lift with him. Once she got down to the Byrne Road bush, the first thing she saw was Crystal Norris on a log by the fire making out with Roman.

Jill's voice rises as she goes into detail about the screaming and yelling that followed. *Two-faced slut! Lying bitch!*

Roman separated them. Jill punched him in the stomach. More screaming.

Mark invited Jill to take off with him, go to another party he'd heard about. But Roman suggested that Jill come back to Crystal's place with the two of them to talk it through. Crystal's parents were out of town. And that's what she actually did. The three of them hiked back along the trail to the road in silence and got into Roman's ugly black Firebird with the shitty gold bird emblazoned on the hood.

"Why didn't you take off with Mark?" I whisper.

"Because! I had to know what happened."

"What happened is: Roman's an asshole and Crystal's a twat. That's what happened."

"You don't know jack-shit, Sammie. You've never had a boyfriend and you've never been in love. You have *zero* life experience. I had to get closure." She states this as if it were a life-or-death fact similar to *I had to get a blood transfusion.*

I keep my mouth shut.

"So, I go over there . . . and we're sitting in Crystal's basement." Jill's voice is slushy with tears. "Roman thought we should have a drink and calm down so he made us all screwdrivers. I was sitting on the couch with Crystal, and I'm like, *How could you do this, Crystal? You even tried to make me jealous of Sammie and it was you the whole motherfucking time!* She starts crying and saying how sorry she is. Then Roman starts telling me that he loves me but it just didn't work out. I'm like, *Because I wouldn't fuck you, that's why! And she would!* I started getting pretty pissed off again, you know, like I was about to start busting some heads. So Roman made us some more drinks."

Judging by the smell of her he must have made them strong.

Then they talked and talked some more and then they all cried. Roman too. The whole thing turned into a big gory love-fest. Crystal said that she loved Jill and Jill said that she loved Crystal. Roman said that he loved them both. Then he made more drinks and there was laughing and tears and hugging. Roman kissed one of them and then the other. Crystal kissed Jill and Jill kissed Crystal and the next thing you know, Crystal and Jill are necking with each other and then each of them with Roman.

"*Puke!*" I say. "How could you kiss Crystal Norris?"

"Crystal's my girlfriend," Jill says.

"Since when do you make out with your girlfriends?"

She pauses and then begins to cry. "Oh God, I can't believe I was necking with Crystal." Jill is really bawling now—heaving and sobbing mixed with these high little squeals.

"Shh." I glance out the back window at the house. The windows are still dark.

A long whimper comes out of Jill. "I'm not a virgin any more."

"You don't mean *tonight?* Holy shit. See! This is why I do not drink. Shit like this. You don't even *like* Roman any more."

"He gave me ten bucks and put me in a cab. Like I was a *hooker.*"

"I don't think people pay for a hooker's cab rides."

"And the two of them stayed there together." Jill is silent for a long second and then she lets loose. "I lost my *virginity!*"

A close-up of Roman comes into my head, his moustache, and his tight jeans and his gruesome hard-on, and the thought makes me gag. "I don't get this. Did Roman force you or something?"

"He said he loved me."

I wince. Suddenly it is clearer in my mind than ever that sex and booze are the downfall of humanity. Drew's *I Love You* echoes in my head. The sensation of his hand on my breast comes back and I scratch the sheet roughly over my chest to make it go away.

"I wonder if my mother did it with Fat Freddy," I say, my mouth twisting up. "She must have."

"What are you talking about?" Jill wails. "Are you *listening* to me?"

I want to kick the crap out of them all: out of Drew and out of Jill and Roman, Freddy and Marlene, Sam and Peggy! All of them fucking while Rome burns. That's the phrase right there. That's what they're doing: Fucking while Rome burns.

Sam pushing Marlene toward the bedroom, Roman telling Jill he loved her—and then the way Marlene and Jill act about it! Both of them in a snit as if they just had something swiped when in both cases they handed it over on a silver platter. I'm supposed to feel sympathy?

I can't stand any of them. All of this bullshit probably has a lot to do with why Sam doesn't call. Except with him it's not booze and sex, it's money and sex. How am I supposed to compete with that?

———

It's light outside but not bright. My watch says 8:10. The sound of birdsong seems really inappropriate right now. I'd be surprised if I slept three hours.

In the cold light of morning, my rage feels a bit broke-down and limp. When a picture of Drew slips into my head again, though, when he takes my hand along the back road in Langley, I pull it away. I fold my arms and keep to myself. I don't want any of it. From anyone.

Jill told me once that there was a rumour going around at school about me. "People notice that you're a bit tripped out about being touched," she said. "A lot of people think you must have been raped."

Apparently the rape rumour started because one of the guys in Jill and Crystal's crowd—probably that idiot, Mark—came up behind me in the courtyard at school and put his hand on my butt. My elbow flew back and nailed him in the gut. He doubled over and bellowed as if I'd just shot him. *Tough titty, don't touch my ass!*

Another time, the same idiot reached for the locket on the chain around my neck and I smacked his hand away before he could touch it. It was a locket that Sam had given me when I was little. And it was right in the vicinity of my boobs, for God's sake.

I had the impression that Jill enjoyed telling me what they were saying about me. As if, not only did she have the inside dope, but she now had more evidence that I acted like a child as well as looked like one. I wonder if she told Ruby all that crap. Jill's big mouth is probably why Ruby keeps on hugging the hell out of me.

I look across the trailer at Jill now. She's still conked out, lying on her side. Only one eye is showing. Her makeup is smeared around it like a bruise. There's a vague stain of purple lipstick on her puffy lips. She stinks worse now than she did when she came home.

She looks like a giant baby, lying there. Except she's not one. Can't even call her a technical virgin now. That seemed to be the worst of it last night: the fact that she wouldn't be able to tell people that she's a virgin any more. She kept repeating it over and over. As if her hymen was the best and most crucial part of her.

You'd think that someone had murdered her family and stolen everything she valued in the entire world the way she carried on. Meanwhile, nobody we know ever believed she was a virgin anyway, not the way she's always strutting around like she knows more about sex and drugs than we'd know in a lifetime. .

I hope to hell she had the brains to make Roman use a rubber, that's all I can say.

Sitting up, I grab my jeans from the end of the bed, haul them on and step into my sandals. Jill wakes. A groan. She rolls onto her back and then back onto her side. She pushes herself up on one elbow.

"Oh fuck. I think I'm going to boke."

"Better do it out the window," I tell her.

She squints up at me, eye shadow and mascara smudges all over her face. "Sammie," she says.

I just look at her.

Her eyes are red and puffy and it seems as if she's about to start bawling all over again. "Swear. Please. Swear to god you won't tell anyone what I told you."

I shrug and shake my head. "Who am I going to tell?"

TWENTY-SEVEN

IT'S ABOUT TWO in the afternoon when I get to the balcony of
our apartment. I was supposed to be here sometime around
noon but I decided to walk from Jill's and the closer I got the
more anxious I got. I stopped at a phone booth on Kingsway
and dialled Marlene. I'm going to be late, I said. Have an errand
to do. Have to pick up something for Ruby.

"That's okay," my mother said. "I'll be around."

The way she said that made me feel sad. Ruby had said that
Marlene sounded good, but maybe what "good" meant to
Ruby was that Marlene had lost her will to kick ass.

I stood on the sidewalk and tried to think of some decent
way to stall. I glanced at the arcade a few doors down but I
can't stand those crummy places. Talk about the ultimate
sucker's paradise: a room stuffed with flashing machines that
scream for quarters.

The Pantry Restaurant was behind me. I thought about going in there and killing time over a cup of coffee. Then again, I was right beside the bus stop. Why not go downtown for an hour, hang out. The sight of Vancouver would probably do me good, remind me of my goal in life: to get the hell out of Burnaby.

The more I thought about it, the better downtown sounded. I could even hit the big drugstore down on Robson Street again. Sitting in the bus shelter, I imagined myself walking into that drugstore, bag in one pocket, receipt in the other, but every time I tried to see it in my head, a hand landed on my shoulder, and that voice echoed in my head again: *Come on, kid. Seriously?*

When the downtown bus finally stopped in front of me, I just sat there looking up at the driver while a wrinkly little man moved slowly down the steps and onto the sidewalk. The driver raised his eyebrows at me but I didn't budge. *Come on, kid. Seriously?* He shut the door and drove on.

Shut up! I thought. Get over it. Shake it off. That hustle was amateur-hour anyway. There are better reasons to get out of Burnaby. Go down to Robson Street and look in the fancy shops, walk all the way down to Denman. Hang out at English Bay.

I imagined myself hopping on the next bus, getting off downtown and kicking around Robson Street without a care in the world. I'd be just turning away from a store window when I'd run smack into Sam.

Fancy meeting you here, I'd say.

He'd be stunned and tongue-tied at first and then he'd ask me if I wanted to grab a bite. We'd go to a restaurant.

Someplace nice. We'd sit down at a table and . . . And I couldn't imagine what then. Sitting in the bus shelter, I worked on witty lines, clever quips that would cause Sam to see me in a way he never had.

Come on, kid. Seriously?

The thought of those words in Sam's mouth made me shudder.

Fact of the matter is, if I were to see my dad on some street like Robson, he'd likely be with Peggy. I wonder if Peggy still boosts, if she's been working her way through those designer shops downtown already.

Marlene told me that people used to place orders with Peggy for exactly what they wanted, right down to the brand name, size and colour. Peggy would make a list and go shopping. That's nerve, boy. I guess that's why Sam likes her.

I must have sat on that bench for an hour thinking about that stuff. Four busses went by, until I realized that I wasn't going anywhere. I finally got up and headed into the Pantry.

It was quiet in there. On Sundays, the Pantry is loaded with churchy-looking types: moms in pastel suits and dads in shirts and ties. The little kids always have shiny patent-leather shoes. I kind of enjoy looking at them. They seem more like illustrations of people than real ones. Happy, shiny people.

I sat down at a booth in the corner and ordered a cup of coffee. As soon as the waitress came back with the cup-and-saucer on her tray, I changed my mind. Before I could speak, she set it down.

"Can I have tea instead?"

She looked at the coffee and let loose a sigh as though she'd just jogged down to Colombia and picked the beans herself.

"I'm sorry," I said. "I don't really like coffee. I forgot."

She came back a minute later with one of those little aluminum teapots and a fresh cup. As she set them down on my table I heard a familiar voice. I cringed, not wanting to be seen.

"Excuse me," I said quietly, trying to keep the waitress near to block me from view a little longer. "Can I have some, uh, do you—Hey, do you have honey . . . dear?"

When I called her *dear* she gave me another one of her world-champion sighs and pointed to a blue plastic bowl at the side of the table with packets of jam and marmalade.

"Should be some in there," she said and walked away.

Glancing around, I caught sight of Jill's poofy hair sprouting up over the back of a booth. Facing her, droopy nose and all, was Roman.

He probably wouldn't have recognized me but I slunk deeper into the booth anyway. I didn't want to talk to them. Either of them. He's twenty-two years old, I thought. Doesn't anyone else find this icky? Doesn't anyone else want to call the cops?

Picking up one of the creamers on my saucer, I peeled back the paper top and poured it into my tea. I put the teaspoon in and stirred a little, then stopped and listened. Couldn't hear a word from Jill or Roman.

Inching sideways on the bench seat, I tried to get a better look. Roman wasn't paying attention to anyone but Jill. His hands reached across the table toward her. His face looked pained. His eyes were red-rimmed and baggy. He leaned forward as though he didn't want anyone else to hear what he was telling her.

The waitress headed over to them. I sipped my tea. It tasted like rust. I glanced at the back of the waitress at their booth, decided I didn't want to be there any more, got up and walked out the door.

Didn't occur to me until I was on the sidewalk that I'd just pulled a dine-and-dash. My heart started to thump. I imagined I heard my waitress sigh. What if she has to pay for it?

Just as I turned back to look at the entrance, she shoved through the door. She looked at me. Her mouth hung a bit as if she didn't know what to say at first.

Finally she said, "Are you taking off? Or what?"

I glanced across the street and then down at my watch, patted my pockets as if I were looking for a smoke. "Um, yeah," I said. I found a crumpled dollar bill. I came toward her a couple steps. "Is that enough?"

She looked down at my buck, then snatched it out of my hand.

I watched as she yanked the door open and went back inside.

I called myself a loser on the waitress's behalf. Kingsway traffic rushed past me, trucks and buses roaring, exhaust pluming. I headed west, in the direction of our apartment. Felt strange to think *our apartment*. Walking toward it, I tried to picture myself sitting in the living room, hanging out with Marlene like old times.

———

And now I'm here. The sliding glass door is open and the tele-vision is on. The sheers are drawn but I can see Marlene sitting on the couch, bent over the coffee table. She's playing cards. Solitaire, it looks like. Since when does Marlene play solitaire?

I can hear a rerun of *Alice* but I can't see it. Marlene lays her cards down uncertainly, as if she isn't quite sure of the order of things any more.

The canned laughter roars and one of the actors yells a twangy, "When donkeys fly!"

Marlene looks up and blinks at the TV and then sets the deck down and picks up a thin paperback and a pencil. Crossword puzzles? She stares at the page and then carefully prints some-thing. Her hands look frail from here, not like the pale, elegant hands I've always known, but pink and bony and raw. If a chicken had hands, they would look the way Marlene's do.

I open my mouth to make some sort of noise to announce myself, but then I stop.

Say something. You can't just stand here spying on her like a goddamn peeping tom.

But I don't. I just listen to the people on television rail at one another in familiar voices: *Stow it, Flo! Kiss my grits!* Big laughs.

I stand still and listen to the catch-phrases I've heard a thou-sand times and all the phony laughter and when the theme music starts up to let me know it's over, I nod a couple of times as if to show that I've been listening, as though somebody flesh-and-blood has been talking to me all this time.

I turn and slip quietly down the cement path and into the alley where I won't be seen.

TWENTY-EIGHT

"THERE SHE IS," Ruby says when I come into the kitchen. "How goes the battle, Sammie?"

Jill is sitting at the table. She looks dreamy-eyed and blushy as if she's just won the Miss Universe Pageant.

I stare at her. She grins. I suppose that she and the Roaming Nose made up today. I wonder if she caught a glimpse of me leaving the Pantry.

"How'd your visit with your mom go?" Ruby asks. She rinses her hands in the sink and wipes them with the tea towel on the counter.

"Fine." I look at the box of French onion soup mix behind her. Ruby's been mixing an envelope of the stuff with hamburger meat in a ceramic bowl. I love that stupid bowl. It's white with these goofy yellow ducks along the sides. Makes me smile every time I see it. Hamburger meat and French onion soup mix is one

of Ruby's favourite recipes. Soon she's going to crack an egg
into that duck bowl and mash it all around, then fry us up some
burgers for dinner. Or maybe Lou will barbecue.

"Well? How was she?" Jill asks in high, gushy voice. "Did
you just hang out or did you go out somewhere together?"

It sounds as if she's got something she wants to say but she's
trying to make a show of giving a damn about someone else
in the room.

"What's going on?" I ask, mostly because I don't feel like
lying. I'd finally called Marlene from a pay phone and said that
something had come up. I'm really sorry, I told her. Will you be
around tomorrow?

"I've got a meeting at six with my sponsor," Marlene said.
"But I'm around in the afternoon."

Sponsor? Took me a second to figure out she was using
AA-speak. The foreign country of Our Apartment now has a
complete foreigner living inside of it.

I look at Jill. "What's with you?"

Jill looks at Ruby and Ruby looks at me.

"Jill has some news," Ruby says on her way to the fridge.

I bet. Jill appears as if she might blast off at any moment.
"Roman asked me to marry him!" Her voice is slurry and
squeaky as if she's drunk with glee.

I glance at her left hand: nothing but bangles on her wrist
and a silver thumb ring. "He actually proposed? With an
engagement ring?"

Ruby walks back to the counter with an egg, cracks it on the
side of the bowl and plops it into the raw meat.

Jill looks exasperated a second before she says, "The *point* is, he said that breaking up made him realize how much he loves me and he wants to be with me. He wants to spend his life with me. I asked him straight up, you mean marriage? And he said, yeah. One day."

Ruby's hands are in the bowl now, squashing the meat and egg together.

"So, you're not actually *engaged*," I say. "You're sixteen."

She looks as if she can't believe what a twat I am and gives me a smile as smug as hell. "There's sixteen and there's *sixteen,* baby. I'm not in the same universe as, say, *you.* Or most girls my age. Can you seriously imagine me dating a sixteen-year-old *boy?*"

Isn't anyone going to say, *Come on kid, seriously?*

Ruby is still kneading the meat. Her face has a funny little smirk on it. The same one she wore when she cornered me in Jill's bedroom five or six weeks ago. Inscrutable chicken: the game that Ruby excels at.

Jill taps a cigarette loose from the pack on the table and lights up. Exhaling, she says, "Can't you just be happy for me, Sammie?"

"A good friend doesn't just say what you want to hear, Jill." Ruby lays a damp tea towel over the bowl of meat and puts it in the fridge. "A good friend tells you her honest opinion."

My eyes flick from Ruby to Jill. I'm such a creep. You're supposed to be excited for a person when she says she's getting married. I should at least act a little happy that she's happy. "Maybe you could just date him again for a while and see how it goes?"

Jill rolls her eyes. "*Obviously,* we're going to be dating. But we have a commitment now."

Ruby sits down at the table. "Did you see your messages by the phone, Sammie?"

I walk back into the hall, glad to escape, and peer at the little pad on the wall with the dangling pencil:

Sammie—Drew called. 12:30 p.m.

Sammie—Your dad called. 3:30. He'll try again tonight.

Drew called and Sam called. Doesn't make sense to see those two names together on the same piece of paper.

Like a wolf and a lamb. It repeats in my head like a nursery rhyme. *Drew and Sam, like a wolf and a lamb.*

"You going to join us for dinner tonight?" Ruby calls. "Lou's gone to pick up buns and lettuce."

I read the second bit on the pad again slowly, word by word as if I'm translating. *Sammie: Your dad called. 3:30. He'll try again tonight.*

It's the wolf you need if you're going to get along in this world. Suddenly I'm tearing up as if there's a cold wind hitting my face.

"Sammie?" Ruby says. "You there?"

Sam is where I'm supposed to be.

"Yes," I say finally. "Thank you."

My eyes move from the words on the pad to the phone and part of me wonders why the hell it doesn't ring. The writing on the wall says it will ring. It should ring right now. I check my watch. What's "tonight" supposed to mean? Is that after dinnertime? Dinner's at six-ish. Seven? Eight? Any old time before midnight? I want to get a chair and sit here in the hall and watch until the phone does what it's supposed to.

———

Dinner drags on for years. I only catch snatches of conversation. I don't make any.

I do hear Lou say, "I thought you said Roman was a loser and *loogan.*"

Jill says she's going to get nail extensions.

Ruby's million-year-old friend Adele isn't doing well. Something about a hospice.

What's a hospice? I wonder. It sounds worse than a hospital. I should be in a hospice. Maybe they'd remove the cotton batting from my head.

Sharp noise cuts through the fog: A chair leg scraping the floor, a car horn, an ambulance siren—every squeal makes me jump, turn in my chair and look toward the phone.

"Don't worry, he'll call," Ruby says.

Oh God, could you quit jinxing me, Ruby? Could you just shut your big trap before you make Sam disappear all together?

———

After dinner Jill gets up from the table and goes downstairs to her bedroom to call her "fiancé." I wash the dishes while Ruby dries. My belly feels like a circus act—as if a family of tightrope walkers is in there, teetering from one side to the other, back and forth. Lou is sitting at the table, staring out the window into the backyard while he pokes his teeth with a toothpick.

I can't hear Jill when she's downstairs. Can't tell for sure if she's still on the phone but I damn well know she is. She'd be back upstairs gloating if she weren't.

Every couple of minutes I look over my shoulder to the hall door that leads down to the basement and Jill's room. Get off the goddamn blower!

After half an hour, Lou picks up the hall extension and says, "Jill, wrap it up. I'm expecting a call." He drops the receiver back in the cradle, stands beside the phone still toothpicking his teeth and then he picks up again and says, "Jill, put the phone down. Now." He listens, says thank you, and hangs up.

He steps back into the kitchen, big and beleaguered.

"Who are you waiting to hear from?" Ruby asks with her little Buddha lilt.

"I'll never know if she keeps talking to that jackass," Lou says, then opens the door off the kitchen that leads to his and Ruby's bedroom, and clomps upstairs.

I love Lou. Lou is the best thing about Jill. He is the best thing about Ruby. What would it be like if Lou was my dad? Who would I be if Lou and I were married?

———

The four of us are in the living room, Ruby and Lou sitting close on one couch and me fidgeting alone on the other. Jill stands by the window and watches the road. The place stinks of her wafting perfume. Jill has had a bath and put on fresh makeup, and blow-dried her hair to never-before-seen heights. Roman said he would be by at seven-thirty or eight to pick her up. It's now nine o'clock.

An old Scorsese movie called *Alice Doesn't Live Here Anymore* is about to come on television. I've seen it before with Marlene. She loves Ellen Burstyn. She loves that movie. I like it too. I guess we sort of relate to it, even though Marlene and I have way more secrets than the mother and son in that show. I wonder what it will be like to watch it without her.

"Why don't you call and see what's taking him," Ruby suggests to the back of Jill's head.

Will everybody just stay off the goddamn horn!

"I'm not calling him," Jill says. "I'm going out." She turns around and looks at me, her arms folded tight across her chest. The gold cross dangling from her neck is caught between squashed-together boobs. "Want to go to a movie, Sammie?"

I look from her to the commercial on the television: a woman in a flowery dress runs, slow motion, through a field. The gravelly announcer's voice says, *Come to find the beautiful fragrance of Jontue: Sensual but not too far from innocence,* as a man on horseback searches for her, his cape flapping in the wind.

"We *are* watching a movie," I say and gesture at the TV as if the show has already started.

Jill glances to the screen as the prince on horseback finally finds the girl in the flowery dress. Romantic music plays as they ride away on his horse together.

She opens the front door and slams it shut behind her. The three of us stare at the television as she stomps across the porch and down the steps. When we hear the tinny slam of the camper door, Lou says, "Hmm. Anyone feel like popcorn?"

At five after ten the phone rings and I dive off the edge of the couch. I'm in front of the telephone before the second ring is finished.

Clearing my throat, I snatch the receiver off the hook. "Hello." My best voice. The low, smooth one that sounds like I'm an expensive secretary.

"Hey, uh, is Jill there?"

"Who's this?" I know damn well, though.

"Roman."

"She left," I snap. I hate him and his fugly moustache and his crappy Firebird. I hate everybody. "Where the hell have you been? You said you'd call! Or be here, or whatever."

"Uh, yeah. I fell asleep. Could you tell her I'm sick."

"Uh, bullshit," I say and slam down the phone.

Everybody's so goddamn full of shit. I want to rip the phone off the wall. I want to scream so loud it echoes from here to hell and back. If I drank booze, I'd chug a hundred bottles right now. If I had sex, I'd fuck a thousand men.

TWENTY-NINE

SOMEONE IS BANGING on the door. Oh Christ, where am I?

It's the camper door. I'm in the camper. I've been dreaming. One of those horrible falling dreams.

"Sammie!" Ruby calls and then she opens the door. "You alive in here?"

I squint at her as if she's a stranger. Can't clear the falling sensation out of my guts. It's hot in the trailer. Airless and still.

"You've got a call waiting for you in the house," she says.

A call? What time is it? Quarter past eleven? Holy Jesus. I've been asleep for nearly twelve hours. Jill's already up and out of here.

My legs swing down and my feet touch the floor. Ruby closes the door.

I pull pyjama bottoms on as the dream flings around in my head: my mother and Drew were a couple. Except that my mother

248

turned into Jill. Jill kept Foxy-Browning all over Drew and tossing her big hair and telling him all the sex-things she'd teach him.
She was twice his size—next to Jill, Drew was just a flimsy bit of
string. They went to bed together, just across the camper on Jill's
side. Suddenly Drew changed his mind. He got up and left her
over there before they could actually do it. He came to my side
where I was pretending to be asleep, and he sat down on the edge
of the bed. He brushed the hair out of my face and said that I was
going to set myself on fire if I wasn't careful. I tried to wake up
enough to tell him that I wouldn't do it with him, but I was so
tired I couldn't speak. Eventually Drew gave up on me. The whole
camper shook as he walked out. It swung sideways and Jill started
to scream. As Drew stepped off the bottom step of the camper,
we tipped over sideways. Parked on a cliff, the whole camper
dropped right off the edge, end over end, falling and falling.

———

Inside the house, I can't shake the off-kilter sense of falling. And
being pissed off with Jill.

The receiver is balanced on top of the wall phone. I don't
want to talk to anyone.

What if it's Drew at the end of the line? I scratch my head
hard and pick up the receiver.

"Hello?" I sound like a toad from the ditch in Langley.

"Hi," Sam says. "You know who this is?"

"No." Hope it hurts him to hear that. I hope it stings his ears
and burns his guts.

He laughs. "It's your old man!" he announces. "What's doin'? Sleepin' late, eh. Guess you're still on summer holiday."

"I thought you were supposed to call last night." I just want him to say it, just say he didn't call and he never intended to and that he's a liar. Or else say he did call and he got a busy signal.

"Sorry about that. By the time I got done last night, it was too late to be callin' over there. Big game. West Vancouver. Lotta money. You got plans today? Can I take you for lunch?"

Holy shit. This is it. Sam wants to meet. We're going to talk. He's telling me about last night's game so I'll understand: he had to make some money while the getting was good, had to set himself up, set us up. He couldn't stop to call.

"Okay. Are you downtown?"

He says he is.

"You want to meet at English Bay?" I know just the place. There's a restaurant by the water. I've walked past it before and looked at the people dining on the patio, first-class people with sharp clothes and long, clean fingers. I imagined Sam and me there one day, looking out at the water and making plans for the future. "The Bay Café? It's down at the end of Denman Street. Near Davie."

"Can you get yourself down here?"

I look at my watch. "How about two? Is that too late?"

Lou should be back way before then. I could borrow his truck.

"Sounds good. I'll be the fella in the pink carnation."

"Ha!" I say. "Ha ha ha!" Just like those little goats in Langley goofing around, that's Sam and me.

My dad laughs too. "Okey-doke," he says. "I'll see you at two." His voice sounds silly and happy. As if he can't wait.

We can't wait!

THIRTY

THE SUN IS smashed open on the blue water like a broken piggy bank. I'm sitting here in Lou's truck, listening to the radio and staring out at English Bay while I wait for Sam to show up. It's still a few minutes before two.

Full of people today. Smart-looking people—downtowners, they look like they know what's doing, who's on the take, and who's a square john. Not to mention the fact that they've got this awesome ocean, for chrissake! Why would anyone want to live in Burnaby if you could just shove over about seven miles and have this?

When Lou got home from work, I told him that my dad called, that Sam and I were going to meet for lunch down at English Bay. Right away he offered to loan me his pickup to get myself here. It's ironic when you think about it: a prison guard lending me a truck to meet up with a guy who's been in and out of jail as many times as Sam has.

When I hung up after making plans with Sam, Jill asked me if I was going to call in to the Pacific Inn to get some hours for next weekend.

"Can't. I'm meeting my dad later. I might not even be here this weekend." I told her where we were going.

"Nice." She looked like she hadn't slept much.

"Did you talk to Roman this morning?"

"He's *sick*," she said. "Fucker better have malaria is all I can say."

Her eyes were a bit sad. I tugged at my T-shirt. "I don't know what to wear," I said. "Maybe you could . . . I mean, you always have good ideas about clothes."

Her face brightened a little. "Um. Sure, I could give you a hand. Come on downstairs and we'll put an outfit together."

I wish Jill could get a load of Sam. Sam always looks good. I wanted to wear something sharp like Sam would—something that would make me look like I was used to being downtown by the water. Urban and stylish.

Jill came through like there was no tomorrow. She was nice to me. Nicer than I was to her yesterday, that's for damn sure. She even offered to do my makeup. I let her do it too, but when I looked in the mirror it was pretty bad. With the summer dress it was like a creepy combination of *Whatever Happened to Baby Jane* and *Lolita*. I said thank you and hugged her. Once I had driven a little way from the house, though, I pulled over and wiped most of it off.

The palm trees wave at the twinkling bay as if I'm some-where exotic. Makes me feel a bit misty, thinking of how nice

Jill was and knowing that after this week, I might not see her again for a long time.

I roll up the windows and take the key out of the ignition, and the truck goes quiet. At exactly two o'clock, I open the huge driver's door, jump down onto the road and slam it shut. How could you not feel like you could take on the world in a righteous black pickup like this?

I snatch a glance at my reflection in the side window and take one more look at the water before I start toward the Bay Café.

I'm wearing a white cotton sundress with eyelet lace on the bodice and at the hem just like you see in *Seventeen* magazine. Jill went through everything in her closet. I tried on a thousand things. If it was Jill's it didn't fit. If it was mine it looked stupid. I was ready to cry, until Jill remembered this dress that her cousin had left in the basement last summer. She crawled to the back of her closet to get it.

Looked awful at first, all mashed up in a plastic bag, but Jill shook it out and pushed me to try it on. It fit pretty well, so she went upstairs and got out the ironing board for me. I was scared I'd wreck it and asked Ruby to do the actual ironing. The next problem was my feet. I didn't have anything that would go. Jill's got major clodhoppers and I couldn't wear anything of hers. A pair of brown suede cowboy boots would have been awesome. That's what the girls in the magazines wear. Boots would have been so cool—I'd be walking with a swagger if I had boots on right now. Instead, I'm heading up Denman Street in a little pair of leather sandals. Jill calls them *water-walkers* because of the way they look like something Jesus would wear.

Ice cream shops and tourist joints line the sidewalks. The air is extra clear and everything looks a little too new and bright somehow, the colour of Playmobil toys. I glance around at the high-rent clothes people have on. When I look down at my sundress, I suddenly notice a yellow mark on the skirt the size of a quarter. Stopping, I lift the skirt a little and take a swipe at it, as if it might just be chalk. It's a stain, though. Something sags in the centre of me. The girl in the stained dress. The girl from Burnaby.

I push myself forward. It doesn't *matter*. Don't be such a baby. Sam and I are blowing this town. We can buy all the white sundresses we want.

Stepping onto the corner where the Bay Café is, I spot my father down the block. He's wearing one of those tailored dress shirts of his, baby blue and starched to cut. That and a pair of sleek tan slacks.

He's coming toward me down Denman Street, and we're an equal number of steps away from the restaurant door now. He matches me stride for stride. When you've got a lot riding on a situation, everything starts to seem like an omen. And this seems like a good one: something about balance, as if Sam and I are both on the same see-saw.

A couple of feet apart, we stop. With the sun hitting him in the face, he shields his eyes. Sam and I are nearly eye-to-eye now. I'm five–seven and he's just a little taller. I flash on Lou ducking as he passes through to the kitchen. Sam ducks cops, questions and ex-wives. But not me. Not now.

I take another step. Stop.

He's tanned. As if he's been in Miami. He raises his arms to embrace me.

Like overstuffed Raggedy Ann dolls, we don't bend in quite the right places. We pat each other's back.

"Long time," Sam mumbles.

It's been almost a year. I wonder if he remembers that shopping trip. I wish *I* hadn't thought of that. Marlene's voice bangs around inside my head: *Come on, Momma. Pushing me into the bedroom. Come, on, Momma, come on . . . Nice guy, eh.*

I look down at a crack in the sidewalk, rock on my sandals and then stumble a bit as I go for the restaurant door. I pull the handle. It doesn't budge.

"Closed," Sam reads.

"How come?" I stare at the door like someone just told me heaven was shut down.

He cups his eyes as he looks inside. "Looks like they're doing renovations."

The both of us search around for a sign to tell us what the hell to do next. Two taxis roll by in traffic.

"You cab it here?" I ask.

"Uh . . ." He looks back over his shoulder. "We're in a hotel down the block."

We meant him and Peggy. At least he didn't bring her along. That must count for something.

"I could drive us to a restaurant in Stanley Park," I suggest.

"You got wheels?" He pops his eyebrows a little and smirks and the two of us turn and head for the truck.

As I step off the curb to cross the road, my knees are suddenly stiff. I wonder if Sam might be nervous too. *More* nervous, like the way people say a spider is more scared of you than you are of it.

He gives Lou's truck the once-over before he gets in. "This belong to your friend?"

"Her dad."

He eyes the dashboard and comments on how new it looks. "What's he do?"

"I think it's leased," I tell him. "He works at Oakalla Prison and her mom doesn't do anything." They're none of Sam's business.

I sit up straight and put the key in the ignition. The engine fires up easy and the full-stomach rumble of it makes me feel better.

"Jill's dad took me to get a road test a few weeks ago," I say. "I just got my driver's licence."

"Jeez and he's lettin' you drive his nice new truck already, huh?" he says.

My father rolls down his window as we drive into the park. "So, how's your life?"

"S'all right. One more year of school. But I talked to the guidance counsellor about finishing early or even in a different city." This part isn't exactly accurate. Crystal Norris said once that she talked to Mr. Walters about finishing early. Sam would like it if it were me who took that initiative, though. "Mr. Walters was saying if I—"

"What's doin' with your mother? She outta that place yet?"

I glance at him. "What place?"

"That mental health place. Your mother give 'em my number, I guess. They gave me a buzz to see if I knew where you were. I gave them your friend's number."

"I thought they called the Welfare to find me." I roll my window down too.

"She out?"

"What? Oh. Yeah. Few days ago. Maybe more."

"You and her are talking, aren'tcha?"

"I went and saw her there." I steer us toward the aquarium and the zoo and glance sideways to read him. Can't, though. No one can read Sam. That's what makes him good. "She liked it there. She said she was scared they were going to send her home and so when she went to group therapy she put green eye shadow all over her face. They acted like it was no big deal. Kept her around another week, though."

He laughs. I do too. Any hustle that works is a good hustle.

"You're going back home, then?"

I keep my eyes on the road. "I don't think she's—"

"Peggy said you had a number for Freddy. I tried calling him and his number's not workin.'"

"No."

"How come you told Peggy you did?"

"I don't have it with me."

"Why didn't you just give it to Peggy when you called. Your mother talks to Freddy still, don't she? I got to get something from him."

"She's—" I was trying to figure how to put it. I didn't want to knock my mother to Sam. *Benedict Arnold.*

As far as he's concerned, the fact that a person would start drinking the way Marlene did in the first place is proof of weakness. If I told him that she was doing AA now, he'd make out like she was the most weak-kneed jerk on the planet. Sam figures if a person's got backbone, he doesn't need a crutch like AA.

I don't like AA either, the way they pour their guts out to one another. But you have to give Marlene credit for making an effort.

"She threw out all her pills and she quit drinking," I say. Then, so he understands it's a real medical condition, I add, "That's how she ended up in the hospital in the first place: grand mal seizure."

Sam looks at me like I'm an idiot. Like, *What's her health got to do with my Freddy shit?*

"I mean she's—" I lean my elbow on the window frame. Sam doesn't need every goddamn detail. "She doesn't talk to Freddy any more. We live in Burnaby."

He mutters something out the window. Then, for a full minute the only noise is the truck's rumble and the swish of trees passing us on either side.

Finally, I ask, "Did you ever actually sell houses? I mean in Toronto. Were you into real estate?"

"Sure," he says. "Cars too. Freddy and I used to fix up these old heaps just enough so's they'd make it around the block." He laughs.

Trilogy of Terror floats through my head. Cross-eyed Karen Black chased around her living room by the Zuni doll. Just four more houses to sell. Three more. I blink at the road ahead.

"You got a lot of games lined up while you're out here?"

"Got a game this afternoon," he says.

"You do?"

He shoots me a look. "Have you got Freddy's number where you're stayin'? Can't you call those people you live with and—"

"Those people don't know anything!"

Hard to say if that came out as loud as it did in my head. I swallow and put a hand out the window, let the breeze cool my fingers.

Out of the side of my eye I can see Sam's mouth purse. He's staring hard out the windshield as if the way ahead might look like a sun-dappled park road to the untrained eye but he knows something different.

When he speaks again, he says, "Things would've been different if I hadn't've gone to jail. I only should've got a few months but they made an example out of me. In the end I did nearly two years."

I watch the road, waiting for him to say something else. My thumbs rub hard on the grooves of Lou's steering wheel. "Mom said if you'd had a decent lawyer you probably wouldn't have done any time at all."

Sam's face sours as if his ex-wife's lame ideas continue to disgust him. "They catch you, you do a little time."

I wonder if he's thinking of me, falling down John Reynolds' front steps, not being where I was supposed to be. "I think about that day and I, I just wish I did things better than—"

"You never shoulda been there," Sam says, and then he starts rambling about Freddy and the truck and I can't follow the story, all the dodging and weaving. He says he tried to offer John Reynolds a few bucks if he would keep the cops out of it. Sam doesn't say what Reynolds' answer was. I guess it's obvious.

"So I told Freddy," he fires on, "'make him a better offer.' What's he do? He offers him some jewellery. Stuff from his *basement.*"

"You and Freddy still work together?"

"I know people everywhere I go. There's practically no city in the country where I don't know someone. In the States too."

"But Freddy's not your . . . Don't you have a regular partner any more?" I glance at him. "Don't you need—?"

He doesn't look at me. Just the road. "I was working with a guy for a while. We played the Granny Game in Los Angeles mostly. A little in Florida. I don't see him no more. He's—" Sam pauses. He swipes at the air as if this guy he used to work with is a lost cause. After a few seconds, he says, "Once we were on our way to a game and he . . . He seen this little girl at the side of the road when we were driving. Twelve years old maybe and he says, *pull over,* and I says, *we don't got time for that,* but he keeps saying how pretty she is and let's pull over . . . I don't know what was wrong with him. She was a little girl."

Another rabbit punch. *Why did you tell me that?* But there's something about the way that my dad just said *little girl,* the tone of it, as if maybe he's using this half-assed story as a way into a real conversation.

Blue water flickers through the thick of the trees and then, just as I'm getting up the guts to ask about us, about him and me and what's going to happen, he says, "Me and Freddy did some work with the Italians in New York. *Those* guys—every time they pass a Catholic church, they're doin' this—" He crosses himself. "And they're *killin'* guys!" He goes quiet again.

Some piece of me is winding tighter and tighter, and then, without looking, Sam asks if I still go to church.

"That was ages ago!" I snap. *None of your business.* I don't want Sam even knowing about that stuff, or Drew or any of those people. "*Welfare* paid for that Jesus camp a couple summers ago, that's all." I hit the word *Welfare* extra hard so he won't miss it.

Sam has no comment. He's an atheist.

"Whatever," I mumble. "It's not my style."

It's true, it's *not* my style. But just as I say that, it suddenly seems sad that I don't see those kids any more, Mandy Peterson and the rest of them. Even that dorky youth pastor. A flash of movie night at Tenth Avenue Divine hits me again, Drew and me giggling in the hard wooden pew.

But I'm not one of them. I don't need them. Doesn't matter because I am right where I'm supposed to be.

I take the next curve on the smooth park road and suddenly the Teahouse is right in front of us.

"This is it," I announce to Sam in a peppy kind of voice, and pull into a parking spot that faces the water.

Sam gets out of the truck. I look across Burrard Inlet and pause. My eyes get hooked on the glow of that heap of sulphur way out in the harbour. A massive mound of yellow powder has been in that spot since forever. When I was a kid I used to imagine tobogganing down the slope and making canary-coloured sand castles and just generally romping around the way little kids do.

I look back at Sam as he walks toward the restaurant, stops and rummages in his pockets. His blue shirt radiates. The Teahouse looms fancy behind him. He'll fit right in here. As long as he doesn't say too much.

Maybe if we just sit down at one of those milk-white table-cloths, our faces reflecting in one of their shiny silver tea sets, everything will smooth out between us.

Shoving open my door, I steady myself to jump down from the truck, and as I reach out to grab the door frame, my dress strap snaps.

"Shit." The white bodice droops down on one side. "Shit," I hiss again.

I grab my purse. Two safety pins hold the ripped lining together. I unhook one of them. In the rear-view mirror, Sam shuffles as he waits. I slam the door shut behind me.

"Dad," I call, and the word feels like a big marble knocking my teeth. "I broke my . . ." I walk toward him, hold up the end of the strap and then smooth it back over my shoulder. "Can you pin it for me?"

He takes the safety pin as I turn my back to him.

The feel of his hands as he fumbles at my bare shoulder blade—trying not to stick me, trying not to touch too much—is more weird than anything else today.

"There." He steps back.

I roll my shoulders to make sure the strap is secure.

Sam looks at his watch. "Jeez, it's late. I told these guys I'd meet 'em at three. Why don't I take you for supper instead?"

It's twenty after two now. I open my mouth: nothing comes out.

"You mind drivin' me to Bosman's Motor Inn?" he asks.

I look at him.

"It's just over on Howe Street." He looks down the park road.

"Sure thing," I say.

I wish my sandals were cowboy boots, big mean shit-kickers with pointy toes and square heels. But they're not, so I spin toward the truck like a dancer instead. I don't think I ever said *sure thing* in my life before today.

I stare at the water and the sulphur as we walk back to the truck, that yellow mountain with no kids on it. It looks different to me all of a sudden. An ugly, wrong type of yellow.

We get back into Lou's pickup and drive out of the park. We don't say a word.

In front of Bosman's, Sam says, "I'll call you later, and we'll go for a nice Italian supper." He digs into his pants pocket. "Listen, give this"—he takes out a folded wad of cash and peels off two hundred dollar bills and two fifties—"to those people you're stayin' with. Give it to the parents. Say thanks."

I nod. He nods.

As he walks quickly toward the motel, I can't get that mountain of yellow sulphur out of my head. Some guy my mother dated when we first moved back to Vancouver explained to me that that stuff was not for playing in, it was for fertilizer and gunpowder and if I were to get close it would stink like rotten eggs.

At Tenth Avenue Divine, the youth pastor said that hell smells like sulphur.

Why would they put that sort of stuff by the water? At the beach. Seems mean to me now. Cruel.

I wipe my eyes, put the truck back in drive and head east.

THIRTY-ONE

A FEW BLOCKS past Boundary Road, I turn down Patterson Avenue and then putter slowly along Sardis until I come to our apartment building. There aren't enough trees to keep me hidden but I suppose there's no point in trying to hide a monstrosity like Lou's truck.

Doesn't matter anyhow. No way in a million years would Marlene expect to see me pull up in a big black pickup.

I ease in along the curb, turn the volume down on the radio and let the engine idle. The curtains are open today and they flutter a little in the breeze.

Leaning forward, I peer at the apartment window. I can just make her out, moving like a shadow from the hall into the living room. She sits down on the couch and disappears from view.

I turn off the ignition, climb out of the truck and lean on the front fender, watching. My head feels blank, as if I could lean here all afternoon trying to put a thought together. What would I say to her if I did go to the door?

I hear Sam's old words in my head: "That's the difference between us and them—the professional works out everything that the amateur has to sweat out. If you got to sweat every move, that's what you call a rough hustle." If he was telling the truth, if he really wanted to teach me something, he would have hauled off and admitted that the whole thing is a rough hustle, this whole damn life.

I rest my face on my purse: one less safety pin and three hundred more dollars. I could get my own car with this if I wanted. I could get a plane ticket.

Two floors up and one balcony over, that unemployed loser with the moustache is out on his patio lounger with a beer, tanning his leathery skin. I wonder if Marlene remembers the night she knocked on his door with a plan to jump off his balcony. I wonder what they said to each other. He doesn't notice me out here leaning on the truck. He's too busy staring into his apartment. Must be watching television because he suddenly sits up and hoots and claps as if he's got a game on.

After another minute or so, I shove myself up off the truck and kick my way through the low shrubs at the back of the building, toward our suite.

The sliding glass door of the patio is wide open. Marlene is leaned over the coffee table again, playing solitaire. The TV is on too, only this time it's an old episode of *The Rockford Files*.

She loves Rockford. After Vegas, I used to wish I could find James Rockford and get him to take my mother out on the town, get him to fall in love with her and make her right again. Rockford seemed like the sort of guy who could do that. Except that there's no such guy. Just some actor named Garner, that's all. The really great stuff always turns out to be phony.

I stand to the side of the balcony and watch Marlene as she picks the crossword book off the couch. She stares at the puzzle on the page and bites the end of a pencil. Her fingernails catch the light. They're shiny, as if she gave herself a manicure this morning. My eyes follow them like fishing lures. Seems like ages since I saw shiny fingernails on my mother. It gives me a little flicker in my throat.

Inside my purse, three hundred bucks are breathing heavy. I put my hands down on the balcony railing and face east, the direction those crows fly home to bed every night.

"It's you!"

I turn around, startled, to see that Marlene has spotted me. She's standing up now, between the coffee table and the couch, hands dangling at her sides.

Inside me there's a rush, like roller-coaster nerves—like hustling nerves—through my arms and down through my guts. My legs get a Gumby feel to them, rubbery and boneless. I keep hold of the balcony for fear I'll fall flat on my face and start bawling.

She comes out from behind the coffee table and moves slowly toward the open door. It feels as if there's a bird thrashing around in my chest, something with a small voice screaming *go go go*—but I keep still.

Marlene reaches the sliding glass door and peers out at me, her eyes big and brimming.

I hold tight to the railing and it's everything I can do to hold her gaze.

ACKNOWLEDGMENTS

I would like to express my sincere gratitude to the BC Arts Council and The Canada Council for the Arts. Their support helped make this book possible.

Big fat squeezes go to Karen DeVito and John Turnbull for their home and hearts and frat room. When the going got hairy, the hairy got going.

And as always, teary gratitude goes to my editor, Anne Collins, for her steely belief that the story is in there. Even if the pot needs to simmer for a while, the story is in there.

BILLIE LIVINGSTON published her critically acclaimed first novel, *Going Down Swinging,* in 2000. Her first book of poetry, *The Chick at the Back of the Church* was a finalist for the Pat Lowther Award. Her second novel, *Cease to Blush,* was a *Globe and Mail* Best Book and her story collection, *Greedy Little Eyes,* was the winner of the Danuta Gleed Literary Award as well the CBC's inaugural Bookie Award for short fiction.

A NOTE ABOUT THE TYPE

One Good Hustle is set in Sabon, an "old style" serif originally designed by Jan Tschichold in the 1960s.

The roman is based on types by Claude Garamond (c.1480–1561), primarily from a specimen printed by the German printer Konrad Berner. (Berner had married the widow of fellow printer Jacques Sabon, hence the face's name.)